A Love

AFFAIR FOR
ETERNITY

BOOK 2

C. Wilson

LETTER TO MY READERS

Y'all harassed me for this release, and I promise you that I got it out as quickly as possible. In my last letter, I told y'all to get a drink or some smoke for this one. The same rules apply. If you need snacks, go and get them now because you're going to end up reading this in one sitting. I want to give a special shout out to the members of my reading group: Cecret Discussionz. Y'all stayed on my ass with getting this one out, and for that, I appreciate you all. Even my little headaches in the group lol. Well, let me stop taking up your time. Get to it, but before you do, I just wanted to say… thank you.

-xoxo-

C. Wilson

A Love Affair for Eternity Book 2 Playlist

Kissin' On My Tattoos, August Alsina

Pieces, Tamar Braxton

Grass Ain't Greener, Chris Brown

Naked- Bonus Track, Ella Mai

Believing in Me, Monica

Love and War, Tamar Braxton

Love Don't Change, Jeremih

Exchange, Bryson Tiller

Do You, Ne-Yo

Butterflies, Queen Naija

None of Your Concern, Jhené Aiko ft. Big Sean

Easy, DaniLeigh

*C*hapter 1

"Hello!"

Tori shot up in her bed and pressed the phone into her ear deeply. The sounds of car horns blaring and loud crashing noises made her stomach uneasy. She looked at the face of her cellphone and saw her sister's name. She had to make sure that the right person had called her.

"Eternity!"

"Everything alright?"

Tori put one finger up for Man-Man to be quiet. She plugged her other lobe with her finger as she pushed the phone closer to her ear.

"Eternity!"

She listened for a response. For anything, perhaps a noise. When she heard nothing, she feared the worse.

"Something isn't right."

She said as she snatched the covers off of her body. Man-Man stopped putting the cufflinks into the cuffs on his shirt and then turned around to face her.

"What's going on?" he asked when he saw the worry lines dress her face.

"I don't know, but it's Eternity. Call Vincent, please."

Tori put her phone on speaker and then quickly stepped into some sweatpants. Man-Man put his phone on speaker as he quickly started to take off the suit that he had just dressed in. His business meeting would have to wait.

"Aye, man, what's up?" Vincent answered on the second ring.

Tori crossed the room quickly and then yelled into Man-Man's phone.

"What happened to my fucking sister?"

There was a silence on the phone.

"Mayne, what da hell you talking about TeeBae? She just called the damn house and my cell. Me and lil man was in here knocked out."

Tori softened her tone.

"She called me, but all I heard was what sounded like metal crushing, I don't know. Something happened to her, I know it."

Tori couldn't stop the tears from falling as she spoke. There was another silence on the phone until Vincent broke it.

"I'm getting the baby dressed. We about to head over to y'all so we can check out these roads."

"We can be out looking right now. It doesn't make sense for you to come over here." Tori said.

"When I say we check these roads, I mean me and Man-Man, you need to stay inside with baby boy."

"Oh NO THE FUCK I'M NOT. She is my sister Vincent."

Vincent sighed.

"Exactly why you don't need to be looking fa nothing. Put Man-Man on the phone."

Tori rolled her eyes and then walked away from the phone.

"I'm here."

Man-Man was pulling a hoodie over his head as he answered.

"I'ma be there in like fifteen minutes," Vincent said.

"Aight."

Man-Man said as he stepped into his black Timberland boots. Once they were on his feet, he hung up his cellphone and then just stared at Tori. She still held her cellphone in her hand. The sounds of sirens filled the room.

"This isn't good," she cried lowly.

He walked over to her and then kissed the top of her head.

"Stop stressing yourself. You're stressing my baby."

Tori gave him a half-smile. Earlier that day, she had just found out that she was pregnant. When she shared the news with him, he was ecstatic. Besides the opening of his new sport's bar, *The End Zone,* Tori being pregnant with his first child was the best news that he had gotten all year. They didn't even know how far she was but that didn't stop them from spending the whole day thinking of the baby in her womb. The sound of an electric saw sounded from Tori's cellphone. She covered her mouth as tears fell down her eyes. Her phone beeped and when she looked down, she saw that her screen said: *Call failed.*

Quickly she picked up her phone and then called her sister. She had to get her again. There was no way that she could handle the call failure with what she had last heard on the phone. When she received no response, she called again. Looking at the frantic expression on her face, Man-Man chewed on his bottom lip. He wasn't the praying kind of man, but he pleaded with God on this one. Silently he prayed that Eternity was alright. He needed Eternity to be alright. He knew that the mental state of his girl depended on it. When he sat beside Tori, she laid her head onto his shoulder. He could tell that she was still crying because the bed lightly shook with each sniffle.

"She gone be good, okay?"

Silence.

He expected it, so he kissed the top of her head repeatedly to try and calm her.

Vincent quickly strapped baby Malik into his car seat. When he closed the car door, he leaned up against it and then looked up to the sky.

"Fuck!" he roared.

At this moment, nothing else but Eternity's safety mattered to him. When she had left earlier, he kept checking his phone, waiting on a call from Nova with information on this mystery man that was in the pictures with Eternity.

All-day that he spent with his son, he questioned it. He wondered if there was a possibility that Malik wasn't his. He spent the day wishing that Treasure had not shown him those pictures as well. Knowing that something might have possibly happened to Eternity had him second-guessing everything. He looked up at the setting sky; the only thing on his mind was her.

He knew that the night would be a long one. He had planned on dropping the baby off to Tori and then scouring the streets for Eternity. If after a while that didn't work, then he would start visiting hospitals. He turned onto Highway 153 and pulled straight into traffic. He sucked his teeth at the bumper to bumper mayhem. The flashing lights on the opposite side of the highway drew his attention. Now he knew why there was traffic on his side because everyone was too busy looking. Like everyone else, he looked at the seven-car, two truck pile up. His stomach went hallow when he saw a silver Audi crumbled. The car looked like foil.

From where he was, he could see that the driver's side door was sawed off. *That can't be her car. It just can't be.* His thoughts were confirmed when he got a glimpse of the dented license plate as he passed by slowly. His eyes watered as he fell back into the flow of traffic and sped up. He was switching lanes to get off on the next exit so that he could get back on the freeway but on the opposite side.

He needed to speak to a fireman or police officer that was still on the scene. He was sure that they would know where the people hurt in the accident were sent. His phone started to ring. When he saw that it was Man-Man, he quickly answered the call by pressing the button on his steering wheel.

"*Yea, mayne.*"

"*Head over to Erlanger Memorial. Tori just got a call. She's there.*"

"*I'm on my way.*"

Vincent gripped the steering wheel tightly and then sped over to the hospital.

Erlanger Memorial
Chattanooga, TN

Tori sat in a chair beside the hospital bed. Her hands held onto the bed's rail. Her arms were stretched, and her head hung in sorrow. Her back heaved up and down, matching the sound of the ventilator.

"Relax…"

Man-Man rubbed her back.

"Mmmmmm."

She groaned as she cried. The pain she felt radiated throughout her body. She lifted her head up. Her face was aligned parallel to the ceiling. Slowly she shook her head from left to right with closed lids. She had to keep more tears from falling. *This shit can't be happening.* She thought as she ignored the sharp pains that she felt in her stomach.

An hour prior, they had started. She just knew that it was signs from her body telling her that she was losing her fetus. If that wasn't a sign, then the wetness she felt in between her legs sure was. But she refused to move and refused to tell Man-Man what was wrong. He would put her needs above her sister's, and right now to her, no one was more important than Eternity.

"It's getting late bae, and you ain't eat shit. You gotta put something on your stomach."

Silence.

"Tori, you need to eat," Man-Man spoke again.

He rounded the chair to stand directly in front of her. Blocking the direct line of what she was focused on.

"Tori... you need to eat," he repeated.

"Okay..."

Her raspy voice was so small. It had been the first word she said since she got the call about her sister.

"Ahhhh, noooo, big baby."

Tori and Man-Man looked to the door and saw Vincent standing in the doorway. He held a car seat with baby Malik inside of it.

"How did this? Is she? What happens now?"

He didn't know what question to ask first, so he stumbled over everyone that came to mind.

"She was pinned up all crazy in the car, so there was some internal bleeding. They fixed that, but she just hasn't woken up yet from surgery. They said something about some swelling on the brain."

Man-Man explained because he knew that Tori couldn't.

"Bring him here, please."

Both Man-Man and Vincent looked Tori's way when her small voice spoke. She held her arms out for her nephew because she needed him right now. He was the closest thing in the room to her sister, and knowing that she couldn't climb in the hospital bed, she needed the love from her nephew. Mentally Tori knew that the child in her stomach was making its exit, and although the doctors were hopeful about Eternity waking up, she wasn't. To her, swelling on the brain never sounded good.

Vincent crossed the room, never taking his sights off of his love in the hospital bed. Her hair was neatly pulled away from her face. She looked angelic despite the breathing tube being taped to her full lips. Vincent placed the car seat in the chair that was beside Tori and then set the baby bag onto the floor in front of the chair.

"Are there premade bottles in there?" she asked Vincent as she pointed to the bag at her feet.

"Yea."

He responded as he reached into a side pocket and then handed her one. She quickly passed the bottle to Man-Man.

"Marcelo, can you please ask one of the nurses is there anywhere that you could heat this up and please send a nurse in here. I have some questions for her."

Man-Man kissed the top of Tori's head before he made his exit. Tori watched as his tall, robust stature swayed out of the room. Every time he walked away from her, she held her breath. Even if the time apart was brief and temporary, seeing him walk away always did something to her. In the short time of them being together, they were so connected. She had caught his vibe and absorbed it whole. Marcelo Bridges made it easy to love him.

She bit her bottom lip, and her eyes watered at the thought of her possibly losing a piece of him. She wondered how she could have possibly fucked that bag up. How could she fumble something as simple as carrying his seed? Still so young and slightly immature, she put the weight of guilt on herself. An older woman would have known not to do that. With age and maturity, other women know that sometimes things are given to you and then taken away before you are even given a chance to enjoy them. That's life. To Tori, she felt like the complexity of pregnancy wasn't complex at all. So, the feeling in between her legs that told her that she was losing life didn't make any sense to her. She sniffed away her inner thoughts when a nurse came into the room.

Vincent walked over to Eternity's bedside. He needed to somehow let her know that he was there. Just how she had stood by him when he was at his lowest point, he was now doing the same for her. Briefly, moments of his recovery while he was in rehab crossed his mind. She was the one that was cleaning up his vomit and then dabbing his forehead with a cool cloth afterward to bring him relief. The same woman that he could have killed with his own two hands was the one nursing him back to sobriety. He totally ignored the nurse's and Tori's conversation as he looked down at the love of his life.

He could say that without hesitation. She was, indeed, the love of his life. Being in his mid-forties, he had never loved. Two women prior to Eternity had conceived his children and still, he could say that he had never experienced what some may call the world's greatest joy. That feeling was foreign until Eternity came his way. *You gotta pull through, Big Baby,* he thought as he rubbed the back of her hand.

"Did you have some questions for me? I can page her doctor if you need me to."

The nurse who had just walked into the room said to Tori with a slight smile.

"This has nothing to do with my sister…"
Tori looked behind the woman at Vincent and then whispered. He seemed to be so into Eternity, so she assumed that he wasn't listening, but she couldn't be too sure.

"I wanted to know if you have any sanitary napkins. I'm pregnant. I know that I'm not any more than a few weeks, but I think that I'm bleeding badly."

The woman's eyes widened a bit.

"I'll go get you some. You should really see one of our doctors here."

Tori ignored the end of the woman's statement.

"Please hurry before the man that came and got you comes back."

Tori's eyes were pleading with the woman. The nurse quickly made her exit, leaving Tori in her thoughts. She knew that eventually, she would have to tell Man-Man about the miscarriage that in her heart of hearts she knew she was having, but right now just wasn't the time. With the focal point on her sister, she didn't want attention from anyone. She wasn't even focused on the well-being of her fetus so to her, no one else should be either.

The nurse hurried back into the room with Man-Man on her tail.

"Aye lady, I know you heard me calling ya ass out there in that hall. I said, did you help my old lady with what she wanted to know about her sister."

"Ohhh, I didn't even hear you out there, and actually, what she needed from me is handled."

She stood in front of Tori with her back facing Man-Man.

"Here you go," she whispered.

Discreetly she handed Tori four pads. She waited for her to put them away into the bag that was seated beside her before she turned around.

"Let me know if there's anything else that I can do." She added before she walked to the door to make her exit.

"Rude ass," Man-Man mumbled, "here, bae." He tried handing Tori the warm bottle, but she started to stand instead.

"How about you feed him while I go to the restroom."

She looked down at the chair she was sitting in to make sure that she didn't leave behind a mess. *Whew,* she thought. Man-Man took the baby from her, and then she grabbed her purse and walked into the bathroom. As soon as she locked the door, she placed her bag onto the sink. She caught a glimpse of her reflection in the mirror and cringed. Her skin looked oily and clammy. A wave of wave nausea hit her. She turned on the water and then placed both hands under the faucet.

When the water pooled into her palms, she splashed it onto her face. She placed both hands onto the sink and then sighed. She just knew that once she used the bathroom that she would be letting her baby pass through. After drying her face and then placing tissue onto the seat of the toilet, she took a deep breath before she popped a squat.

She looked down into her panties that were now placed at her calves. *Nothing.* She filled the bowl with her urine and quickly wiped herself. *Nothing.* She expected to see blood coming from her body, but there was none. *So, being pregnant gives me the juice box, huh?* She thought of the wetness she had been feeling in between her legs for the last couple of hours. The ringing of a phone caught her attention. She tapped the pocket of her sweats, but her phone wasn't vibrating with the ringing. She looked at her purse that was sitting on the sink.

"Fuck," she whispered.

After pulling up her panties and sweats in one swift move, she rushed over to her purse. She dug around inside of it to try and locate the phone, but the ringing had stopped. She had forgotten that when she arrived, the doctors had given her Eternity's belongings. Besides Eternity's screen now being cracked, her phone was in perfect condition. Since the ringing had stopped, she quickly washed her hands and then dried them. She went back into her bag to look for the phone. Tori had finally retrieved it to see that there was a missed call.

Malik

She read the name of the caller over and over. *Should I tell him about her?* She chewed on her bottom lip in thought. Overstepping her boundaries, she felt like she had to. She was about to excuse herself out of the room to call Bleek from her cellphone.

When she opened the bathroom door, she saw Vincent gently wiping Eternity's face with a damp cloth.

"You gone push through big baby. You the strongest person I know."

Even with his back facing her, Tori could tell that he was crying by the way his voice cracked with each word. *Fuck! I know she gone wake up. She has to. She can be the one to tell me if she wants me to call.* She took a seat next to Man-Man and watched as he burped the baby over his shoulder. She smiled, thinking about their product in her stomach.

Chapter 2

"Yo bro, they are making the last call to board."

Sha watched as Bleek stood in the middle of the walkway. His narrow eyes were fixated on security clearance. His bushy eyebrows dipped as his dark pupils scanned the crowd of people. Desperately he was hoping to lay eyes on *her*. If he saw a glimpse of her in that crowd, he would make sure that the plane remained grounded until she made it to the gate. He repeatedly patted the extra boarding pass he had into the palm of his hand.

"Fuck…" he growled, "aight let's go."

He walked past Sha and then handed the attendant his boarding pass.

"Have a nice flight Mr. Browne."

His response was none as he made his way onto the plane.

As soon as he boarded, he sat into his first-class seat. The empty seat beside him ate at him. Eternity and her baby were supposed to fill the space. Per stewardess request, he put his phone onto airplane mode and then fastened his seat belt. The plane cruising down the airstrip getting ready for takeoff didn't feel right. It felt off. Something in his soul was telling him to stay. When the plane started to rise, he knew that it was a little too late for that.

He sighed deeply and then relaxed his head onto the headrest. Just when he was about to catch some sleep, he felt the presence of someone next to him.

"Can I have a word?"

Bleek opened his eyes and then looked at Sha without responding because he knew that his boy was going to speak his mind regardless.

"Maybe… and I could be reaching, but just maybe this chick you wrapped around just likes playing these games."

Bleek gritted his teeth together at the mention of Eternity. He had just opened up to Sha about her on the way to the airport, so the last thing that he wanted was *his* opinion on the situation.

"I don't know her, but from what you told me, y'all been doing this back and forth thing for a while now. It's leaving you distracted. We still need to figure out who robbed us last Christmas Eve. You gotta get ya head back and stay focused."

Bleek listened to every word and silently agreed with him. He had been off his game. Ever since Eternity had come back into his life, everything about him was irregular.

He couldn't understand how the makings of her threw him off his shit every time. Every single time. The glimmer in her eyes when she was around him made the stars look dull. He saw her at her worse point and still found beauty in her. Still, he loved her. His love ran so deep to the point of pain. The more he tried to love on her, the more it hurt. Especially on days like this one, days where she would stand him up. He was rough around the edges, but his heart was golden. *That gotta mean something, right?* He thought as he cupped his beard with his strong hand and then gently rubbed his facial hair.

He was officially sick and tired of the games. Love that felt like this made you weak and vulnerable. There was no way that after all these years in the game unscathed that he would let the blindness that comes with love be his downfall. He had a friend that let love be his weakness, which led to his demise. There was no way that he would allow that to happen to him.

"As soon as we touch down, we will get to business."
The gaze that Sha saw when he looked Bleek in the eyes when he spoke satisfied him. That cold icy stare let him know that it was time to put it work.

"Welcome back, boss."
He patted Bleek's shoulder before he stood up and then walked back to his seat across the aisle.

Bleek took his phone out of his pocket and then started to play Candy Crush. When thoughts of Eternity came because of the game, he deleted the app from his phone and then rested his head onto the headrest once more. While pushing thoughts of her to the back of his mind thoughts on getting to the bottom of this robbery plagued his mind.

※※※※※※※※※※※※※※※※※※※※※※※

Bleek walked through the door of his condo and felt empty. All of the weight of pain he was carrying when it came to Eternity was still there, but he was just numb to it. He figured that he would go home and get some sleep after his flight, but his mind was disturbed. He had been avoiding going to his house because all of the gifts that he had purchased Eternity from the last Christmas was still there. When Connor, his assistant, offered to clean out her things, he denied the service, but now he needed it.

He sighed as he dragged his suitcase across his hardwood floors. Once he put his bag into his bedroom, he walked right back out the door. The only thing that would soothe his mind was his gun range. He had made it across town in no time. He was taking this one day to get his shit straight. The need to check his mental state was mandatory. There was no way that he could get on his grind with his thoughts overwhelmed like this.

After he parked his car in his garage, he was greeted with the two henchmen that stood guard on his property — all protocols to ensure his safety. Instead of walking into his home, he took the scenic route to his gun range that was on the land behind the house. As soon as he unlocked the door by using the keypad, he hit the lights. He went into his office and took his glasses and ear gear out of a case that was hung on the wall. After going to his gun arsenal, he chose his favorite, a Sig Sauer P320.

He grabbed a box of ammunition and then went to hang up a target. He was a great shooter, and that was because he never let his skill go without training. He connected his phone to the Bluetooth speakers as he set himself up.

Bitch I got the Mac or the 40
Turn a bitch to some macaroni
Tell me how you want it I'm on it
I really mean it I'm just not recordin'
Still a blow the choppa, for all you actors
Leave a bitch nigga head in pasta

With his target hung, his glasses, and ear protection on, he aligned himself with the target. Those movie thugs would have gunners out here with their gun cocked sideways. They had young men out here losing their lives because they didn't understand how fatal holding and shooting a gun that way could be.

One of the quickest ways to get your gun jammed is shooting that way. A rookie shooter wouldn't have the skills that Bleek had to get out of that situation. They wouldn't know how to clear that error in under a second to save their own lives, but Bleek did. Thorough, so thorough in the streets, yet he stood in a booth releasing his anger in the form of bullets all in the name of love. He hummed among to Dej Loaf's song as he stood shoulders straight, feet planted firmly on the mat beneath him with his knees slightly bent.

With his finger on the trigger guard, he rested it there until he was ready to shoot. Patience. So many thugs lacked that which lead to an early demise. With his sights lined perfectly and with the stance of a killer, he started to let his slugs rip through the hung paper man. All seventeen shots were headshots. It looked like a slug from a shotgun tore at the target the way all of his shots hit the same spot.

Quickly he dropped the empty magazine onto the floor and then reloaded a new one. After racking back the gun and loading one round into the chamber, he focused on the chest area. On a timer, the target moved, and he followed through each shot with skill. He tossed another empty clip to the ground and then reloaded. When his arms grew tired, he placed the gun down onto the booth's surface and then sighed.

The pleasure he would typically get from shooting didn't come. *What the fuck am I supposed to do?* He questioned to himself. What the fuck was he to do? Someone who was once so emotionally detached now felt everything. She made him feel it all. *I gotta tighten the fuck up.* He thought as he pressed a button on the remote to bring his target in.

Satisfied with his work, he began to clean up the range. After sweeping up his shell casings, he locked up the range and then walked back over to his home. He stood in his driveway, debating on if he wanted to drive back to his apartment or not. *Baby steps.* He thought as he walked over to his car and then pulled out of his garage. Seeing all of the things that he had purchased for Eternity would bring his progress back two steps. Because it was so early in the morning, he made a mental note to call Connor and have him move all of the items into one of the spare bedrooms.

His cleaning crew had gotten rid of all of the Christmas décor, but those damn clothes were still lingering around. Those damn clothes that he knew she loved just by the glimmer she had in her eyes when she saw them. Those damn clothes that, even after almost a year, still held her scent in them from her trying every single piece on. So, for now, staying inside of his home wasn't an option because the simplest thing like lying in his bed was now ruined because thoughts of her consumed him.

Walking into his condo, he started to feel the effects of his travel. He walked into his master bath and then ran a shower. He needed to get that gun smell off of him. He stepped into his shower and then closed the glass door behind him. He rested one of his hands onto the glass wall and then placed his head under the showerhead.

Beads of warm water bounced off his scalp. He just needed a moment to think. So much felt overwhelming to him. He rarely took the time just to stop and reflect. Breathing deeply, he sighed before he moved his head from under the water and then wiped his eyes. After quickly washing, he dried his body and then grabbed his bathrobe off the back of his bathroom door.

Once his body was securely wrapped in it, he walked back into his bedroom. The morning's sunrise was beginning to peek through the blinds. Where everyone else in the city was probably getting up and getting ready for work, he was calling it a night. He put his phone on do not disturb and then got comfortable in his bed...

"Why do we have to keep going through this?"

Bleek sat at the end of his bed as he watched Eternity move around his room. She walked in and out of his walk-in closet, packing her belongings.

"Hello?"

Silence. She said nothing as she put her clothes into her suitcase. He rubbed his hand over his face and then dramatically sighed.

"I need to leave. I can't stay here."

Her voice was just above a whisper. She stood in the doorway of his closet. He rose from his bed and then walked over to the entryway.

"You are trying to leave because you're scared. What you are feeling is what you are supposed to be feeling. That feeling is how you know a nigga is doing right by you. That butterfly feeling in your stomach and that anxiety in your chest is what you get when you fuck with a real nigga. Stop running from love."

She brushed past him as if he wasn't just speaking. He grabbed her hand and then turned her to face him.

"Ma, don't make me chase you. I'm so tired of chasing you. Just be mine."

"I NEED to go! It's like I can't stay."

"Eternity I am so tired of hearing thi—"

Bleek stopped speaking when right before his eyes, she vanished.

"Eternity!"

He poked his head into the closet to look for her, but he saw nothing...

Bleek jumped out of his sleep. He wiped the sweat off his forehead as he breathed deeply. Looking around his room, he saw that the sun no longer peeked through his blinds. He leaned over and grabbed his phone from the nightstand. *Damn, I slept for a long ass time.* He thought as he cleared the missed calls from his notification screen. His heart was still racing from the dream that he had.

As he was trying to analyze his dream, his stomach started to growl. Seeing that it was too late to order food for delivery, he knew that he would have to drive to an after-hours spot to get something to put into his stomach. He got up from his bed and then walked over to his closet. He stood paralyzed in the doorway as the dream that he just had consumed him. He could have sworn that he smelt her scent. Could they have been so connected that at that moment, he felt what she was feeling? He started to wonder if she was hurt. *I can't let this shit be my problem anymore,* he thought. It took everything in him to switch the focal point of his thoughts.

He shook his head from side to side to rid himself of the thoughts of Eternity. Quickly, he grabbed a pair of gray sweatpants with the matching hoodie off of his top-shelf. After getting dressed, he grabbed his wallet and car keys. He drove around the city for a while before he found what he wanted to eat. A bar in the city with the best wings was still open. He found parking right out front.

As soon as he walked into the dimly lit corner street bar, he found his way to the bartender.

"Is the kitchen still open?" he asked as he took a seat on one of the bar stools.

"Mm-hmm, it's about to close in twenty minutes, though. You want something hun?"

Bleek looked at the menu behind her head that hung on the wall.

"Yea, let me get some hot wings with a basket of fries to-go."

"What size?"

"The twelve-piece please and a Corona while I wait."

She gave him a warm smile and then scurried off to the back to put in his order. She came right back and placed his beer onto the countertop.

"I forgot to ask if you wanted a lemon or a lim—"

"Yessssss, girl! You did that!"

The loud voice of a woman cut the bartender off. Bleek turned around to see where the commotion was coming from.

"My girl, my best friend, passed her bar exam!"

"Yesss, I did that shit!"

He watched as the chocolate-colored woman threw her head back with the shot of light liquor that she was taking. He watched as her facial expression twisted with the burn from the alcohol, and then quickly, he turned his head around. *Out of all of the bars in Miami, I walk into one with her in it.* He tapped the bars tabletop as his thoughts consumed him.

"How much longer for the wings?" he asked the bartender.

"Let me go check for you, hun."

The woman disappeared into the back again. Bleek tried to listen to the women in the corner booth talk, but between their squealing excitement and their visible drunken states, he couldn't make out what they were saying.

"Here you go, love."

The bartender placed a plastic bag with his food onto the countertop. He took money out of his wallet and then handed it to the woman.

After taking the final swig from his beer, he put the empty bottle onto the bar, grabbed his food, and then turned to leave.

"Aw shit, I'm sorry."

She had walked right into him. Her basket of fries and wings spilled in between them.

"I am really soooooo sorry."

She continued as she used the napkin in her hand to wipe the stain that she had created on his hoodie. When she saw that she was making it worse, she stopped. This whole time he didn't say anything. He just watched her as she drunkenly tried to clean his clothes. She looked up at him for the first time since bumping into him.

"Malik?" she questioned.

"Hey, ma."

Paris Shaw looked just as good as he remembered, if not better. Her chocolate skin looked soft to the touch, and it was. He had first-hand knowledge of her body. Every frame he touched he learned inside and out. That was the ambition in him to be the very best.

Slap!

Bleek ran his tongue along the top row of his gums and tasted blood. She went to slap him again, but he grabbed her wrist.

"Make that your first and last time doing that."

He said sternly as he threw her arm back towards her, which caused her to stumble backward drunkenly. He grabbed her at the waist to catch her before she fell.

"You wanna tell me why the fuck you just slapped me?" He asked when she regained her balance.

"You went missing on me."

"I did what now?"

Bleek was confused. Things with him and Paris so was good. That is until it wasn't. When she had come into his life earlier that year, she was like a breath of fresh air. With her upbringing being totally different from his still, they found a way to connect. Where he felt like his life was complicated and all over the place, she made it seem as simple as 1+1. She was amazing and definitely wife worthy, but she had a lot of growing up to do. At first, he chalked her slight immaturity and insecurities up to their age difference. He was four years her senior.

"You went missing. We had that one argument and then—"

"And then you left my apartment and told me to forget about you. Did you forget that?" he finished for her.

"You were supposed to follow behind me. You were supposed to—"

"Wrong. I'm a grown-ass man, and this ain't them cheesy ass shows and movies that you be watching. Why the fuck would I chase someone that doesn't want to be caught?"

Bleek lowered his tone because he felt like he was being louder than he intended to be. He knew that his thoughts were right when he looked over Paris' shoulder and saw that her two friends were now eyes glued on him.

"Paris, are you alright?" one of her friends asked.

Bleek sucked his teeth. He appreciated the girl's concern, but he hated nosey people. Paris turned around to address her friend.

"I'm fine, Jessica," she sighed out before she gave her attention back to Bleek.

He was trying to grasp his cool and keep it because he knew that the real venom behind his words wasn't even meant for her. All of the words that he was speaking to her, he wished that he could say to Eternity. He looked down at her and saw that she was looking around nervously. She used her manicured fingertips to move her curly tresses from out of her face and to behind her ear. Easily he saw that he had offended her, bruised her ego. Instantly he felt like shit because from what he had overheard today was a day of celebration for her, and there he was borderline ruining it.

"Look," he softened his tone, "go ahead back with ya girls. Congrats, Ms. Paris Shaw, the lawyer. You're doing good following behind ya pops footsteps."

He had turned to walk away, leaving her wondering how he had heard about her passing the exam in the first place.

"He asked about you, you know?" she said with a slight smile.

"Oh, yeah? That's cool."

He gave her a weak smile and then continued to walk out of the bar. She let him, watching him walk away, was feeding her curiosity. She wanted to stop him, but then she quickly remembered that she was out with her friends.

Bleek walked into his apartment. He had to put his food into the microwave to heat it up. The run-in with Paris caused his food to get cold. He stood in front of the microwave and watched as the food circled under the light bulb. Something about their encounter had him stuck, and she was definitely on his mind. She was naturally glowing. That glow that comes with success always looks different.

When they were dating, she was on her grind for the exact moment that she was now celebrating. He was genuinely happy for her. The beeping from his microwave brought him out of his thoughts. After grabbing his food, he made his way to his bedroom. A vibration noise caught his attention. Then is when he realized that he had left his phone inside the house. He placed his food onto his nightstand and then picked up his phone.

Paris: Uhh... I really wanna sit diwn wuth yoi and talk

Paris: If thos isn't Malik, sorry...

Bleek chuckled at the text messages that he got from Paris. *Her drunk ass,* he thought as he responded quickly.

: Call me in the morning when you're sober

He put his phone down on the nightstand. After peeling off his clothes, he sat in his bed, turned on his television, and then ate his food. He heard his phone vibrate again. When he looked over to the nightstand, he saw that she had sent him a smiling emoji. He shook his head as he thought about the slap she had delivered to his face. Although he was pissed off, he found it incredibly sexy.

Chapter 3

Eternity stared at the Christmas decorations that hung from the ceiling in the physical therapy room. Her son's first Christmas was just in two weeks. This pushed her to regain full strength in her right ankle. Without the support cane that was provided by her doctor, she walked with a limp. She knew that another surgery was needed on the damaged area, but she wasn't rushing towards another scalpel just yet.

Since waking up from her coma, she was surrounded by love from her sister, Vincent, and Man-Man. This physical recovery was already a lot on her plate and as of late, she was starting to feel suffocation from her loved ones. She was questioned continuously about what she remembered from the moments leading up to her accident. Her eyes watered as she held onto the support beam and slowly staggered towards the other end of the room.

She always told everyone that she didn't remember anything when in all actuality, she remembered it all. The impact of the 18-wheeler smashing into her was still so vivid. Random moments in her day, she heard the crash in her head, the metal crushing, and she felt it all. The pain that radiated through her body when her car was hit from several directions was unimaginable. Every impact she felt up until she passed out from the pain, that is. She also remembered her hours before the accident. *I am supposed to be with him right now. S*he thought as she closed her eyes tightly.

She wanted to keep the tears at bay, but involuntarily, they slid down her flushed cheeks.

"Ms. Washington, are you in pain?"

The physical therapist stood at the end of the support beams and watched as Eternity slowly made her way towards him. When she didn't respond to him, he crossed the room to get to her. As soon as he stood directly in front of her, she let go of the support beam and then cried into his arms.

He awkwardly held her. For the past two months, she barely spoke words to him, so he was shocked at the situation that he was now in.

"Are you in pain?" he asked again.

Her back heaved up and down, and loudly, she sniffled onto his shoulder. She opened her mouth slightly to speak, but whimpers came out instead.

"Ayeeee, what tha hell done happened to my lady, man? Big baby, I told you to stop pushing yourself."

Vincent entered the room with a raised eyebrow. Eternity's arms were tossed over her physical therapist shoulders with her hands clasped closed behind his neck.

"Ah-hem," Vincent cleared his throat once he was close enough to the couple.

The physical therapist raised his arms towards the ceiling and then attempted to take a step back. When Eternity leaned further into him, Vincent intervened. He took her arms off of her therapist and then stood in his place. The glare Vincent had in his eyes as he watched the therapist exit held fire in them. He softened his demeanor when he saw that Eternity was still crying.

"Big baby, you in here pushing yourself again."
She shook her head from left to right, which caused her forehead to rub onto his shoulder.

"I just miss Malik…" she whispered.

"Awww big baby. You're coming home today, so we gone swing by Man-Man and Tori's spot to pick him up."

Eternity nestled her face into the crook of his neck and then cried harder. She was happy to be around her son because the time spent with him made the pain that she felt from being away from Bleek hurt less. On a daily basis, she battled with her inner thoughts of leaving Vincent and just going to Miami. The way he put her needs above his own during her time of recovery made her push the notion towards the back of her mind every time.

"Come on now, big baby, let's get up outta here."

Vincent put one arm around her waist and guided her to her coat. He had already loaded the car with her things.

When they made it outside, the chill from the December's wind stung Eternity's face. After Vincent helped her into the passenger seat, he quickly jogged around to the driver's side and slowly pulled into morning traffic. He was careful not to go too fast because of Eternity's newfound anxiety. It took him double the amount of time it usually would have taken to reach his destination, but he finally had made it to Man-Man's house.

"Come on big baby, let's go get our bwoy."

"Can you just go in and get him. The next time I want to get out of the car is when we're home."

Vincent gave her a weak smile and then nodded his head up and down.

Eternity watched as he slowly entered the home that was now her sister's too. When Tori opened the door for Vincent, Eternity saw that she was wearing a plush house robe with the matching slippers. Eternity tried to wave and leave it at that, but a sigh escaped her mouth when she saw her sister approaching the parked vehicle. She rolled down her window to listen to the earful that she knew Tori was about to give her.

"Now, I know your ol limping ass did not pull up to my house just to sit in the car."

Eternity rolled her eyes before she responded.

"Today isn't a good day, Tori. I literally had to do a therapy session right before I got discharged. I'm in pain."

Tori lightened her tone. Quickly she pulled her robe tighter across her body to block out the cold chill from outside.

"Mmm… well, sorry, I thought you were acting stink or whatever…" she crossed her arms across her breast with a slight attitude.

Ever since Eternity had woken up, she had become distant. Her sister was always her go-to, but with so much harbored inside of her, she locked down her mind and kept all of her feelings inside. The silence had become awkward, so Tori prepared to make her exit.

"You might as well come in. Vincent is in there talking Marcelo's head off," Tori said in a welcoming tone.

"Na, I'm alright right here, ToriTee," Eternity said dismissively.

"Well, alright then…"
Tori shook her head in disappointment and then turned to walk away.

"I'll call you when we get home and get settled in."

"You won't, but it's okay…" Tori responded as she made her way back into her house.
Eternity rolled up her window and then reached into her coat pocket. She pulled her cellphone out of it. With her eyes fixated on the front door to the house, she quickly skimmed through her contacts.

She hovered over *his* name and toyed with the thought of pressing the call button. Tori had informed her two months prior when she woke up that *he* had called the night of her accident. Still fresh from her foggy coma haze, she declined that Tori inform him of her condition. Eternity realized now how much of a mistake that was when she remembered the last day she had saw him. The look of hope filled his eyes, but she could also tell that if she didn't make it to that airport that he would be done. She stared at the front door to the house and waited a few more moments.

Trying to guess when Vincent would be walking out that door with her son, their son, was giving her a headache. She had stayed with Vincent these past two months because she felt like she owed him. Even after seeing the condition that the accident had left her in, he stayed at her side. He catered to her every need even when her snappiness enticed him not to. For two months, that is what she drilled into her head, which kept her feet planted in the state of Tennessee. Not until recently did she start realizing that if she would have let Tori call Bleek that he would have done the same. In her heart of hearts, she knew that the love Bleek had for her was unwavering. There wasn't a mountain he wouldn't climb or a sea he wouldn't swim across to be there for her.

She was pissed with herself that it had taken her this long to get it through her thick skull. Before the accident, she would have never thought about shaking the boat called Vincent and Eternity. Now, she wanted to tip the shit over. Her reasoning had nothing to do with how she was being treated because how she was being handled now, was the best she had been cared for throughout their entire relationship.

Her heart that used to bleed with love for the man was now dry and cold. She didn't love him how she used to, and she was no longer into the fashion of forcing that part of her to be revived. She now felt like she was giving CPR to a dead situation. Every time their relationship had flatlined, there she was on the sidelines with the defibrillator, waiting to give life to their relationship again.

If the accident she was in taught her anything, it was that life was too short. You could be here one second and then gone the next. She didn't want to spend another moment away from who she knew she was destined to be with. After this call, she would just have to find a way when they all got home to break things to Vincent. The phone ringing in her ear caused her to chew on her bottom lip.

"Hello?" a woman answered in a whisper.
Eternity pulled the phone from her ear and then looked at the name to make sure that she had called the right person. Instantly her stomach went hallow. She looked at the time on the radio of the car and saw that it had just turned noon.

This relaxed her rushing mind some being that it could have been somebody at his mechanical shop answering his phone.

"Hi, can I speak to Malik, please?"

"He's kind of busy right now can I take a message?"

Although the woman was still whispering, her voice was very professional.

"Uhhh yeah. Just tell him that Eternity called and for him to call me back, it's urgent."

"Okay, will do…"

The line ended in Eternity's ear. She figured that she would let a couple of hours go by before she called again.

Chapter 4

Bleek slowly pulled the condom off of his soldier and then tossed it into the toilet. He put one hand onto the wall in front of him to hold him up while he used the other to drain his python.

"Shitttt," he hissed while he used the restroom.

Once he finished, he flushed the toilet and then walked over to the sink to wash his hands and brush his teeth. His mind was troubled with the dream he had. For two months, it seemed as if he kept having the same dream every night — the dream where Eternity disappears right before his eyes. Toothpaste created foam around his full lips as he scrubbed. He stopped when he thought he heard his phone ringing but then finished brushing his teeth when he didn't hear the noise anymore.

Once he was done handling his morning hygiene, he opened his bathroom door and was faced with the chocolate beauty that was laid in his bed.

"Good morning," she said with a smirk.

The morning was, in fact, good for both of them. Morning sex always put Bleek in a great mood and he needed the distraction. Especially with the dream he had the night before.

"Good morning, did my phone ring?" he asked as he made his way over to the nightstand.

He used his fingerprint to unlock his phone.

"Na, that was my phone ringing," Paris said quickly.

Bleek checked his call log and saw that the last call he received was from Sha the night before. Knowing that they both had the generic iPhone ringer, he brushed it off.

"Oh, aight…"

"Are you ready for your flight to D.R?" she asked, changing the subject.

"Yea…"

Paris raised her eyebrow at his shortness. This morning he was off, and she didn't know why. *Does he know that I answered his phone?* She thought as she watched him tap around on his phone. She almost caught an attitude just thinking about the woman she just had a brief phone conversation with. *Eternity.* Without knowing the face, she knew the name all too well. For the past month, since she had been spending the night with Bleek, it was the same name that he would call in his sleep. She shook off her slight frustration because, in her mind, the woman was no longer a problem. *Got that ass on the blocked list now,* she thought before she spoke.

"Well… I'm about to get outta here, I guess. Unless… you changed your mind and want me to take you to the airport like how I offered last night."

She stood from the bed and started to walk towards the bathroom to handle her hygiene. In nothing but her birthday suit, she strutted, which caught Bleek's attention.

"Mmmm," he groaned as he watched her dimpled ass jiggle with every step.

She got to the doorway of the bathroom and then looked over her shoulder to look at him.

"So… can I drop you?"

Bleek locked his phone and then looked at her.

"I thought you had something to do today. My flight leaves in three hours."

"Well, what I had planned can get pushed back if I want to take *my man* to the airport."

She looked at him and waited for him to correct her. When he didn't, she smiled.

"We can leave as soon as I get out of the shower."

She said, not taking no for an answer. She closed the bathroom door behind her and then went to handle her morning ritual.

Bleek sat on the end of the bed as he waited for her to come out of the bathroom. Since the two had started dating again, she would toss the *my man* title around, but he would always correct her, which would somehow lead to an argument. He didn't feel like arguing this morning. The change in mood that it would cause would only ruin his vacation.

This trip to the Dominican Republic, to Ty's estate, was one of the rare occasions where it wasn't business-related. He went out there every holiday but this Christmas it was more than just about the tree and the presents. Kelsey, Ty's mother in law, was getting married. Not wanting to attend the wedding alone, he thought about asking Paris to accompany him, but he changed his mind when the reality of her not knowing that part of his lifestyle had come into play.

He was due to be gone for only a few days, but he made sure to put Sha up on game to his upcoming vacation. Although he had no worries, he still had to let it be known that he expected no errors in his absence. While Paris showered, he finished packing some of his things. *I need just to leave some shit out there.* He thought to himself as he stuffed his clothes into his Galarché duffle. So many trips to the Dominican Republic, yet he was excited as if it was his first time going. Being around his right-hand man would always do it to him. Florida was his working grounds and New York was the hood but being around Ty and Toya was home.

"You ready to go?"

Paris broke him from his thoughts. He looked towards his bathroom and saw that she was fully dressed in the velour sweatsuit that he had purchased her. Slowly, she was starting to break him down. A man that went from buying nothing for a woman if their name wasn't Eternity would randomly pick up things throughout the day for her. The corners of her mouth turned up into a smile when they made eye contact.

"Yea, I'm ready…"

He said as he watched her move around his room as if it were her own. Quickly she picked up some of her items and then tossed it into her overnight bag.

Bleek chuckled to himself because he remembered times where he dreaded seeing those bags. When he would have women accompany him in his condo for a nightcap, all of them would come with one. Seeing that satchel over their shoulder was a bag of hopes to him, but every single time he would send the women on their way as soon as the condom was off.

"What's so funny?" Paris asked with a smirk.

Quickly, Bleek wiped the smile from his face.

"Nothing…"

He didn't know when he and Paris had gotten this deep into the dating, but he was starting to welcome it. It felt good to have the support that a relationship comes with finally. On days where he worked hard, she would come over and make him feel better. She was that listening ear that always brightened his mood when she spoke. Still, she knew nothing of his street side. She knew Malik, the owner of several mechanical shops. She didn't know Bleek, the King of the east coast.

After grabbing his bag off of his bed, he put on his coat and then made his way to the front. Paris followed. He held the front door open for her while he put his security code in. After locking up, he followed Paris towards his elevator.

"Shit..." he mumbled lowly, "hold the elevator I forgot something."

Bleek stepped off of the elevator and then walked back to his apartment. He quickly turned off his alarm and then picked up the garment bag that was draped over the back of his couch. He put the alarm back on his door and then made his way back to the elevator.

"How you almost forget your suit when you're going to a wedding?" Paris asked as soon as he stepped back into the steel box. Bleek nervously chuckled, "I don't even know."

He wasn't a fan of weddings. The last wedding that he attended was Ty's, and that was just a visit to the courthouse. The wedding that he would be attending now was bound to be a big event. He knew Ty's mother in law all to well. Kelsey wanted nothing short of extravagant. The ride to the airport was starting off as a silent one. Paris turned up the music and then started to sing along to an old Monica tune.

The corners of Bleek's mouth turned upward as he watched her. Every note she missed, and her pitch was off, but she was happily singing as she weaved in and out of traffic.

"I look at you, looking at me. Now I know why they say the best things are freeeee..."

She looked over to Bleek and sang. As she went along with Monica, she leaned over and rubbed his arm as she continued to sing.

"How you changed my world, you'll never know. I'm different now. You helped me growwww..."

Bleek watched how she slowly moved her head from side to side as she sang. She was so into the song that she visibly agreed with the lyrics. Paris caressed Bleek's arm with one hand while steering the wheel with the other, which made him feel uncomfortable. He saw how she was deeply connecting herself with those lyrics. Those words were so familiar to her, relatable.

He turned the song down as they pulled into the terminal.

"Let me know when you land."

She told him more than asked. With all of the traveling he had been doing since they started dating again, she worried every time he left. Bleek got out of the car. With his hands at his sides, duffle bag clasped in one hand, he waited. Once she was in arms reach, he reached for her.

A smile spread across her face. He leaned down and then scooped her into his arms. Slowly they rocked side to side as they shared the embrace.

"I wish I could come with you," Paris admitted.

"Yea…"

She gently shook her head at his response, but she brushed it off. Emotions with Bleek was like pulling teeth for Paris. He showed them but only when he wanted to, which was rarely.

"Well… let me get out of here."

She broke their embrace at his request. She watched as he disappeared into the revolving glass door.

$\mathcal{C}$hapter 5

Bleek exited the airport with his duffle bag in one hand and his coat in the other. Like planned, a black suburban was parked waiting for him.

"What's up, José" he greeted the driver.

"Hey, hermano. Didn't expeck me aye?"

Bleek chuckled as his heavy Dominican accent.

"Na, I did. I know that Tony's wedding is tomorrow." Usually, when Bleek visited the Dominican Republic, his ride to the house was always Tony.

"Yeaaaa, a married man, huh?"

"Yep, he about to be a married man," Bleek confirmed.

He sat back into his seat and then enjoyed the rest of the ride to Ty's estate. When they pulled up to the iron gates, José put the code in. Being so used to visiting, Bleek was unfazed by the six-man army that stood on the grass with assault rifles. They were all sworn to protect the owner of the land they all stood on. *This nigga really be on some drug lord shit,* he thought to himself. Bleek had his own little two-man army at his estate, but it was nothing as drastic as what Ty had. He completely understood though. If he was a married man with children, he would provide the same exact protection.

Once he was let out of the car, he grabbed his duffle bag and then opened the front door to the house. He knew that it would be unlocked. With so much armed security on the land, the front door could have been off the hinges, and still, the Barnett's household would have been protected.

"Fammlayyy—"

Bleek dropped his duffle bag, coat, and garment bag to cover his eyes as he stood in the foyer of his best friend's home. He could hear feet running up the stairs.

"Damn B, why the fuck you ain't call when you got off the plane," Ty asked from the top of the stairs.

"Man bro, I swear I ain't see shit. I umm José was waiting for me at the airport already."

"You can uncover ya eyes now. Shit, I'm dressed."

Bleek slowly lowered his hands from his eyes and then looked to the top of the stairs. He looked down at the bottom of the stairs and then scrunched his face up. He couldn't unsee Ty and Toya's naked bodies. They were so wrapped into one another when Bleek had walked through the door that they didn't notice that they had an audience until it was too late.

Just wearing basketball shorts, Ty walked down the stairs and then held his hand out to dap Bleek.

"You a fucking fool if you think I'm dapping you up after I literally just saw where those fingers were," Bleek said with a straight face.

Ty busted out laughing at Bleek's expense. He folded his arms across his broad chest when he saw that Bleek wasn't budging on the handshake.

"Where my nieces at anyway with y'all nasty asses?" Bleek asked as he picked up his belongings, "y'all asses made me wrinkle my damn suit." He added.

"The nanny took the girls out. Let me head upstairs, though. I know Toya's ass is probably mortified."
Ty turned around and then jogged lightly up the stairs. Bleek shook his head from the image that was stuck there. He climbed the stairs and then walked to his room in the house.

When he got upstairs, he saw that everything in the room was exactly how he had left it. After hanging up his garment bag and coat and dropping his duffle bag into the chair in the room, he sat on the ottoman that stood at the foot of the bed. He took his phone out of his pocket and then quickly sent a text to Paris, letting her know that he had landed safely. He scrolled through his contacts and then stopped when he got to Eternity's name. His thumb hovered over her contact as his mind turned in thought.

Although he was still detoxing her out of his system, he wondered how she was doing. Deep down inside, he knew that he shouldn't have, but he had too. He clicked on her name and then shot her a text message.

: I hope all is good with you, E. A nigga missing you like crazy...

When the text bubble went from the standard iPhone blue and turned green, he knew that his number had been blocked. He shook his head in disappointment and then locked his phone. After he got himself together mentally, he made his way downstairs to see what there was to eat in the kitchen.

He walked into the kitchen and saw Ty and Toya seated at the island.

"The nanny is bringing back food when she comes back with the girls," Ty said to Bleek — knowing that his friend had only come downstairs for food.

Bleek sighed and then took a seat across the island from them.

"What's up sis," Bleek said to Toya.

"Hey…" she said flatly.

Bleek rose his eyebrow at her dry greeting but then shook it off. He figured that she was uncomfortable with what he had seen when he had come in earlier.

"What's up with you?" Ty asked Bleek.

He eyed him as he saw his change in mood.

"This wedding tomorrow, y'all know weddings aren't my thing."

"Well, I told you that you should invite a lady friend," Toya added just before she stood from the stool.

Tyshawn lightly slapped her behind.

"Tyshawnnnn, cut it out," she whined before she hurried out of the kitchen.

"What's good with y'all. Y'all out here acting like teenagers… ew."

Bleek asked once Toya made her exit.

"We were going through a little rough patch, you know how making up is," Ty said with a smirk.

Bleek rubbed his hand over his beard because he could somewhat relate. The making up whenever Eternity would come back into his life was all too familiar to him. The only thing is that she never seemed to stay. That making up is what had him still in Lala land wondering if the baby he had seen a few months ago was his.

Scenes of their version of making up played in his head as he thought of the possibility of that child being his. Then, he remembered how quickly she denied the paternity. Still, he had some sense of hope. So much hope that he had started to put money into a secret account for the child just in case. Now that he knew his number was blocked, he knew that it was time to put all of the questions he had for the past couple of months behind him.

"Yo, you ain't hear me?" Ty asked as he snapped in Bleek's face.

"Na… what you said?"

Ty sucked his teeth because he hated repeating himself. Anyone who knew him knew that.

"I said, why didn't you invite this girl you been dating to the wedding?"

Bleek rubbed the surface of the marble counter before he spoke.

"I invite her, and then what? She sees the damn army you got out on the front lawn. Somebody crack's a joke about selling fucking drugs and then what? And then what…"

Ty tilted his head to the side as he listened to Bleek talk. He, himself, had never been in a situation where his woman didn't know the lifestyle that he lived. He didn't understand why Bleek didn't put the new woman he was dating onto game, but it wasn't his situation to understand.

"You need a brighter mood. Call her and tell her to get on a flight. I'll tell the men on the yard to dial back a bit. You need to unwind and really get the gist of this dating shit, bro. How you dating somebody but holding back parts of your life that made you who you are today? I'm not saying let her know that you a damn dope boy overnight, but you can expose her to the lifestyle in increments."

Bleek listened to Ty intently. Although he didn't want to, he silently agreed with his bro.

"Plus, Toya could use some female company. She hadn't had any since the last time Tone came out here with his wife. Make that call," Ty added just before he stood from the stool he was sitting on.

After briefly stretching, he just stared at Bleek.

"What?" Bleek asked.

"I gotta talk to you about something before you leave."

Bleek raised his eyebrow and fixed his mouth like he wanted to say something, but he didn't. Ty made his way out of the kitchen, leaving him in his thoughts.

*C*hapter 6

Bleek sat in the car and waited on Paris. After the talk that he and Ty had in the kitchen, he decided to give her a call. Knowing that the function she would be traveling for was a wedding, she made sure to pick herself up a beautiful dress for the occasion. She was able to catch a flight out to the Dominican Republic that night. He hoped that Paris and Toya would hit it off because if they didn't, it would make his stay even more uncomfortable.

He looked out the windshield when people started to exit the airport. As soon as the lights outside landed on her soft chocolate skin, he saw a glow. He stepped out of the car to take her suitcase from her.

"Hey you…" she cooed as soon as she laid eyes on him. Bleek pulled his bottom lip in between his teeth and tilted his head sideways as he observed her. Her thighs looked like they could rip the seams of the jeans she wore. This woman was all woman, and he was infatuated with the thickness of her frame. He lightly shook his head from side to side as he smirked.

"What's up, ma."

A simple gesture caused her to show her full set of pearly whites. Bleek loved the slight gap in-between her two front teeth. It gave her character.

After loading up the car and getting in, Bleek started to make his way back to Ty's estate. Twenty minutes into the drive, Paris began to make conversation.

"So, are we staying at a hotel or at your brother's house?" she asked.

"My brother's house."

"Do you think that his house will have enough room for u—" She stopped speaking when she saw Bleek turn onto the property. He brought the vehicle to a stop so that he could put the code in to get past the gate.

"Does this look like enough room?" Bleek asked with a smirk.

He parked in the driveway and then got out of the car. All of the men on the lawn were tending to the grass. Lawnmowers were going off, and plants were getting watered. He didn't see an assault rifle insight and for that, he was grateful. Being so street savvy, he could point out exactly where every gun was though. Paris dragged her suitcase behind her as she followed Bleek towards the house.

"Come on," he said lowly when he noticed that Paris was hesitant with walking through the front door.

He held his hand out for her, and she grabbed it. Nervous shit. She was nervous because she hadn't met any of Bleek's family. She hadn't even met a friend of his. Bleek himself was nervous because this was all new to him.

Bringing around a woman was out of the norm. He chewed on his bottom lip anxiously because, on the one hand, he didn't care what Ty and Toya thought of Paris, but on the other, he wanted their approval. With courting Eternity, he knew that he would never get that approval from Ty, so after a while, he stopped looking for it. Bleek made his way to the kitchen and then into the backyard. Kelsey and Tony were laid out on the grass playing with Ty's daughters while he and Toya were seated in chairs drinking.

"Ah-hem," Bleek cleared his throat to make his presence known.

Ty leaned his head back in his chair so that he could see behind him. When he saw that Bleek was back with his girl, he turned around and spoke.

"Hey, y'all come and sit down."
Bleek dragged Paris to a chair and waited for her to sit before he took his own seat.

"Paris, this is my brother Ty, and this is his wife Toya," Bleek introduced.

"Hi," Paris said with a slight smile.

"Girl, knock all that shy shit out, you drink?" Toya asked as she stood from her seat.

"As long as it's something light…"

"Come with me," Toya said as she started to walk towards the bar outside.

Paris looked to Bleek, and when he nodded his head, she followed behind Toya.

"Does Toya know that she doesn't know about what we do?" Bleek questioned once the ladies were far enough to be out of earshot.

"She knows to monitor what comes out of her mouth." Ty took a sip of his Corona and then continued.

"You feel better now that she's here? Don't you?" Bleek looked over at Toya and Paris at the bar, and a slight smile spread across his face. The two women were smiling and obviously enjoying each other's company.

"A little bit…" he admitted.

"Well, that's something. Let's enjoy the rest of this night. Here," Ty passed Bleek an open Corona.

"Thanks," Bleek said just before he took a swig.

Chapter 7

Bleek rolled over in the bed, and instantly his head started spinning. He knew that he had to get him and Paris up and ready for the wedding, but the migraine that he had was pushing down on his eyes was making it hard for him to get out of the bed. He turned over and looked at the other side of the bed to see that it was empty. Paris stuck her head out of the bathroom door and then looked at him. Her toothbrush was in one hand while she was wiping her face with a wet cloth with the other hand.

"I was going to let you sleep a little while longer before I woke you up to get ready for the wedding," she said with a smile.

He looked at the clock on the nightstand then sucked his teeth.

"Shittt," he hissed, "ma I was supposed to be up an hour ago. I'm in the wedding I had to be up earlier."
He said as he pulled the covers off of his body.

"I'm sorry I didn't know."
Still, he had much time to spare. He walked towards the bathroom, and when passing, he kissed her on top of her head.

"It's cool, ma."

After making his way around her, he ran his shower water. By the time he got out, Paris had his suit laid out for him as well as her dress. Naturally, she was showing him that she had the traits of wifey. Paris was the type that would pull out an iron board and iron. Though she was young, her parents had been married her entire life, so she picked up on these traits from her mother. She worshiped her parent's relationship, and to her, they were goals. She hoped that one day she could experience that same bliss.

"Thanks, ma," Bleek thanked her as he put his underclothes and deodorant on.

In no time, they were both dressed and making their way to Tony's estate. With the same exact layout as Ty's house, Bleek followed the same routine of waiting at the gates to be let in. Once the gates opened, he found a park next to the other cars and then made his way into the house with Paris at his side. People carrying flowers walked past him quickly and then made their way into the backyard.

"Bout time you made it. You had me practicing with one of the damn workers," Toya said with sass as soon as Bleek walked into the kitchen that led the way into the backyard.

"Well, good morning to you too," Bleek said with a chuckle.

"Yea, yea… good morning y'all." Toya said with an attitude.

"Magdala, can you take Paris with you to the yard to sit with *the other* guest?" Toya asked a Spanish woman walking past carrying a baby.

"Okay, Mrs. Barnette."

The woman waited for Paris with a smile. Paris leaned up and gave Bleek a kiss on the cheek. She wiped the lipstick mark from his face and then followed the woman into the yard.

"What was that about?" Bleek asked as soon as Paris and the woman exited the kitchen.

"Nothing," Toya said with a shrug.

The way that Toya was dismissive towards Paris was bugging him, so he had to ask again.

"Na sis, what the fuck was that about?" he whispered into her ear.

"I'll put you up on game later," she said quickly.
Music started to play, letting the wedding party know that it was their time to walk. Toya looked behind her and saw that Ty and Kelsey were in deep conversation.

"Psst... you ready?" she said to her mother.

"As ready as I'm gonna be," Kelsey said nervously.

"Come here, baby," Toya crouched down to be leveled with her toddler, "when you walk down the aisle, you have to put the petals down nicely, okay?"

The little girl in the white dress with curls smiled brightly and then shook her head up and down eagerly.

"Okay, mommy," she said just before she headed out the door and started to walk down towards the aisle.

The little girl walked down the aisle, and with each step, she tossed flowers everywhere. She had yet to learn the finesse that a flower girl was supposed to have. When she got to the end of her path, she ran over to Magdala, the nanny, so that she could sit next to her sister.

Next to walk was Bleek and Toya.

"Tell me what happened last night. Why are you treating shorty like that?" Bleek whispered as they started to walk down the aisle.

"I said later," Toya whispered back.
Bleek started to walk down the aisle quickly. He was practically dragging Toya down the runway.

"You walking too fucking fast," Toya mumbled as she playfully slapped Bleek's arm.

"Man, ya damn feet just too fucking little," he teased back. He knew that Toya would confide in him what occurred the night before, but he had to mess with her for making him wait. Toya walked to her spot on the bride's side while Bleek stood on the groom's side. When the piano changed the tune, Kelsey and Ty started to walk down the aisle.

Bleek watched as the pair made their way to the altar. He heard sniffles, and when she looked to his left, he saw that Tony was crying, and Julian was consoling him. *This why I hate fucking weddings,* he thought to himself as he silently cleared his throat. When he looked into the crowd, he saw nothing but Ty's and Julian's workers. The only family to the couple getting married were in the actual wedding party. He locked eyes with Paris. When she smiled brightly at him, he gave her a smirk.

Under the sun's light, she looked breathtaking. Her natural hair was wet and shrunken into coils that ended at her jawline. Bleek watched as she put the strap to her dress back onto her shoulder. The entire morning while they got dressed, she complained about the same straps that she had just fixed. She was openly expressing her nerves around his family, and he assured her that she was perfect. Bleek knew that no one was perfect but if that was what needed to be said to ease her worries, then that's what he was going with.

Little did she know, he was fully intrigued by her. He was fascinated with her flaws and all. He loved to see her naked and not in the physical aspect. Although he liked that too, he loved to see her in her natural element. He loved to see her at moments where she worried about the strap to her dress falling, and he loved it when she fussed about the way her tresses would lay. The slight insecurities that she harbored about herself were part of the makings of her and he silently was grateful that he was able to witness it. All of this he thought of as he watched her. Closely he observed her. He could tell that she was nervous by the way she switched in her seat.

"Antonio Rivera, if you take this woman, Kelsey Greene, to be your lawfully wedded wife, then say I do," the officiant said, breaking Bleek from his trance.

He turned his head to watch the ceremony.

"I do," Tony said without a doubt.

"Kelsey Greene, if you take this man, Antonio Rivera, to be your lawfully wedded husband, then say I do."

The officiant looked at Kelsey as he waited for her to respond.

"I do," she said.

The couple put the rings onto one another, and then the officiant introduced them as the newly married couple. When they shared a kiss, the entire party clapped for them.

"Eyesa married woman now," Kelsey said as she tossed her arms in the air.

"Ma, I told your old ass not to say that. You are so damn embarrassing," Toya complained as she shook her head in shame. Bleek and the rest of the wedding party chuckled at the mother-daughter interaction. A woman with a clipboard walked up to the wedding party and let them know that the backyard was now ready for the reception.

"The backyard is ready for you guys to eat, drink and dance," she said before turning on her heels and leading the way.

Paris made her way to the center of the aisle to walk with Bleek. Arm in arm, they made their way to the backyard. As if he could smell the food from where he stood, Bleek's stomach started to growl at the mention of it. Bleek felt someone grab his right arm as he walked.

"Follow me, bro. We gotta chat," Ty whispered into his ear. Bleek stopped walking and then looked over to Paris. The smile that she was wearing for no reason started to fade slowly.

"What's wrong?" she asked.

"I need to go chat with my brother for a minute. You think you gone be good in the yard by yourself?" he asked.

"Uhh, yeah… I'll sit with Magdala, I guess."

"Why don't you sit with Toya?" he quickly asked. Since Toya had yet to tell him what had occurred between the two the night before, he was hoping that Paris would.

"Uhhh, it's her mother's wedding. I know she's going to be busy."

Bleek looked at her with a raised eyebrow, but he decided not to push the topic.

"Aight, I'ma be right out."

While Paris walked to catch up with Magdala, Bleek followed behind Ty closely until they made it back into the house and into a conference room. As soon as Ty turned on the light to the office, he sat at one end of the oak table, Bleek naturally sat at the other end. Once Bleek's back was rested into the seat, he spoke.

"What's up boy boy?" he asked, trying to read Ty.

"I'm out," Ty said.

"Out?" Bleek questioned, "what you mean?" he sat up in his chair and then placed elbows onto the table.

"It's time for me to pass the torch to you. I'm leaving the game alone."

Bleek sat back as he listened to Ty give his reasoning as to why he was finally done with the game. He got lost in his thoughts as Ty spoke. He knew how to move weight up and down I-95 effectively, but he questioned if he had what it took to be the plug. Without even knowing it, he was engaging in conversation with Ty although his thoughts were taking over him. When he finally gained focus back into the discussion at hand, he only caught the ending of what Ty said.

"So, are you relocating out here?" Ty asked.

"Naaa… D.R. isn't my speed, bro. I know old ass Tony gone die in this game. I'll let him handle the product out here."

Ty gave Bleek a smile because he could see that Bleek was going to have everything running as smoothly as he did.

"Alright, let's go and enjoy this night," Ty said as he stood from his seat and then walked to exit the room.
Bleek stood and followed him towards the exit.

"I just got a question for you, bro," Ty asked Bleek as he stood in the doorway.

"What's that?"

"Are you ready to be king?"

"I been ready boy boy…" Bleek said with no emotion.

For years he was ready for the throne. He thought that he would have gotten it when Ty had fallen to the justice system, but it just wasn't his time yet. The two men chuckled and then made their way to the backyard to engage in the party with the other guest.

$\mathcal{C}$hapter 8

"Hey you," Bleek said with a smirk as he sat next to Paris.

"Hey," she cooed as she smiled brightly.

"Everything go alright with your brother?" she asked just before she took a sip of her champagne.

"More than alright. Damn, you couldn't make me a plate?" he asked as he stood from his seat.

"I didn't know how long you would take. I'm sorry."

"It's aight…"

Bleek started to walk over to the buffet to make himself something to eat. He was piling food onto the plate in his hand when he looked at the end of the table and saw Toya fixing plates. Quickly he rushed to that end of the table.

"You gone tell me now or what?"

The smile she had when she was talking to the guest in front of him faded when she looked his way. She waited for the people in the line in front of him to walk off before she spoke.

"She just gives me this weird-ass feeling. Plus, she doesn't know how to hold her liquor."

Toya smacked her lips together after her statement.

"What the fuck happened last night?" Bleek asked.

"She just showed that she's insecure. Instead of asking me about your and Ty's history, she was too busy asking me about our *sisterly-brotherly* relationship."

Bleek turned around and looked towards the table that Paris was sitting at. She smiled at him, and he smiled back then he quickly turned back to Toya. His smile faded instantly.

"I'll talk to her about it."

"Mmm-hmmm," Toya said as she added salad onto his already full plate.

After grabbing some napkins, he made his way back to the table that Paris sat at.

"You think you got enough food?" she teased as she watched him sit his plate onto the table and then take the seat next to her.

Without saying a word, Bleek started to eat. He was giving himself time to gather his words. The insecure shit. It was the same reason they had parted ways the first time they tried this dating thing. He hoped that with time that she would have gotten better with it, but what Toya had just told him let him know that she hadn't.

"I like how they decorated the ceremony with blue and silver. Especially since Christmas is in a few days," she said to him to try and make small talk.

"What happened between you and my sister last night?"

He sat the fork that he was just eating with into his plate and then looked her into her eyes. She chewed on her bottom lip as her eyes scanned the backyard.

"Stop looking around the yard for answers. I asked you the question."

Paris looked Bleek in the eyes as soon as he finished his statement.

"I honestly, don't remember much. I was drunk and—"

"You know that drunk shit is never an excuse with me. What happened between you and my sister last night?" he asked again.

"I kind of pried a bit—"

"A bit?" he said sarcastically.

When she looked away, he lightened his tone.

"Look, if you can't get this insecure shit under control, I don't know where we gone go, but I do know that it ain't gone be far."

She looked him in the eyes when she heard the seriousness in his tone. After his statement, he finished eating his food as if the conversation just didn't happen.

"I'm sorry..." she said, barely audible.

"Don't be, just do better."

Paris smiled because Bleek had so much patience. She was a runner, and in this relationship thing, he stayed rooted. Paris needed a man like him to teach her. Still, she lacked the knowledge of sticking things out. Still so immature, she would kick up problems and then run as soon as things got bad. With him, she was learning to work through issues. He was growing her ass up, and she was grateful for it.

"Damn, I wish I didn't have to leave tomorrow," Paris said with a sigh, "are you sure you don't want to spend Christmas with me at my parents' house?"

"I'm sure…"

Bleek noticed the disappointed expression on her face.

"It's not because of last night either. It's just been a while since I spent the holidays out here. I used to come every holiday, but the past year I was held up with work."

Paris smiled at his response. She understood because she knew that he worked all the time.

"Okay…"

"What you can do before you leave tomorrow is make it up to me tonight."

He leaned over and then kissed her neck. She giggled and then watched as he picked up his plate and then stood to go throw it in the garbage.

Paris looked to her side and saw that Toya was walking past.

"Toya…" she called out.

"What's up?" Toya said as she placed a hand on her hip. She still had her Brooklyn roots embedded in her, and it showed in her aura. She was obviously annoyed and made no effort to hide it.

"I wanted to apologize for last night. I was way out of line. The last thing that I wanted to do was get off to a bad start."

Toya softened her stone facial expression.

"It's cool. Thanks for the apology."

"Everything good?" Bleek interrupted.

"Yea don't bring ya ass over here with the worried look," Toya teased.

Toya and Paris shared a chuckle at Bleek's expense.

"So y'all got jokes?" He asked playfully as he took his seat.

"Well, I'll catch y'all later. I gotta make sure my mother and Tony make it to the airstrip on time for their honeymoon."
Toya walked off, and when she did, Paris yawned.

"Don't start that tired shit. You're getting dick tonight."
Paris started to laugh in the middle of her yawn. She stood from her seat and then gave him a seductive look.

"Well, then, I think it's time for us to leave this shindig, huh?"
Bleek pulled his bottom lip in between his teeth and then smirked.
After finding Ty, Bleek told him that he and Paris were going back to the house.

$\mathcal{CC}$hapter 9

As Bleek drove him and Paris back to the house, he thought about the night ahead of him. He needed the extra days out in D.R. It was nice having Paris around, but he was looking forward to her going back home. He would send her back to the states worn out. With the night ahead, he had intentions of being deep in her guts. The wedding had him in his feelings. It had him re-evaluating his love life. He and Paris had too much to work on, so the altar wasn't even an option. It wasn't something that he could see in the near future, and well, he and Eternity were non-existent.

When he felt Paris' hand in his lap, he left his thoughts. Her hand ran over his manhood, and through the polyester material of his slacks, she felt his soldier quickly grow.

"We five minutes from the house," he growled.

"A lot can happen in five minutes, Mr. Browne."

"Sssss," Bleek hissed when he felt Paris pull his member from his slacks.

He sped to the house the rest of the way while she showed off her fellatio skills. When they arrived at the house, she put him back into his pants and then exited the car. *This damn girl yo,* Bleek thought as he situated himself before making his exit.

Knowing that no one was inside, Bleek kissed Paris from the yard to his room. As soon as they made it to his room, he closed his room door behind him. Paris came out of her dress and underwear and then laid across the bed. Bleek took his wallet out of his slacks, grabbed a condom, and then held the wrapper in between his teeth while he got undressed.

He stood in front of her just as naked as the day he was born. She admired his physique. His chocolate skin and washboard abs had her biting her bottom lip as she eagerly waited for him to secure himself and then enter her. The sound of his phone ringing stopped him in the middle of him dressing his soldier. He pulled the latex down to the base of his dick before he went to answer his phone.

"Really, Malik?" Paris asked in an annoyed tone.

"It might by Ty or Toya…"

He said as he finally retrieved his phone.

When he saw that a New York number was calling him, he ignored the call. *I told these niggas to call Sha and that I was on vacation,* he thought as he shot the call to voicemail and then walked over to the bed. Paris was smiling brightly because she was excited to get split in half. Since she reached the land of the Dominican Republic, she was yearning for his touch. The way he maturely handled her fuck up from the night before only made her want it more. Bleek was a man, a grown man, and she was quickly learning that in order to keep up with him that she was going to have to boss up.

As Bleek put one knee into the bed, his phone started to ring. He looked over to the nightstand and saw that it was the same New York number calling again. *Something gotta be wrong.* He thought as he answered the phone.

"*Hello.*"

Paris sucked her teeth as she watched him answer. She noticed how his once erect manhood quickly lost life.

"*Can I speak to her? Okay, okay. I'll be there by tomorrow morning.*"

Paris watched a coldness appear in his eyes as he spoke on the phone. When he hung up, he looked at her.

"Get dress. We need to head back to Miami."

Paris tilted her head to the side. Completely lost, she couldn't understand why their trip had to come to an abrupt end. She watched him slide the condom off of his dead member and then toss the rubber into the nearby trash. Quickly he dressed in his drawers and then threw on a sweatsuit from his bag. He turned and looked at her. In an instant, his thick eyebrows scrunched in anger.

"GET UP and get dressed!"

Paris jumped out of bed and then tossed on clothes. Stunned by the base in his voice, she didn't say anything. She didn't know what had shifted the mood within Bleek, but something in her told her that she didn't want to be on his bad side.

Bleek rushed through the airport with Paris trailing him. She struggled to keep up. When they made it outside, he found the first taxi that he saw and then put her in it. She scooted over in the backseat to make room for him, but instead, he closed the door shut.

"You said *we* needed to get back to Miami, and we're here. Why aren't you getting in the car with me?" Paris asked after she quickly rolled down the back window. Bleek went to the passenger side and then tapped on the window. When the driver rolled the window down, Bleek handed the man two one-hundred-dollar bills.

"Take her where she needs to go, okay?"

"No problem, brother," the man responded as he took the crisp bills from Bleek's hand.

"Malik…" Paris called to get his attention.

"I needed to get *you* back to Miami. There's something else I need to do."

She looked at him with pleading eyes. She tried to read him, but she couldn't. He looked stressed. The lines that dressed his forehead let her know that he was troubled.

"I will call you okay?" she said to him.

He nodded his head and then stepped back so that the car could pull off. So many thoughts swam around in her head. She wanted to be there for whatever it was that he was going through, but the distance that he showed their whole trip home let her know that it wasn't wanted.

Quickly Bleek walked back into the airport. He needed to be on the first thing smoking to Tennessee. After getting himself a flight that was due to leave in about an hour, he grabbed a seat and waited. When his phone started to ring, his stomach went hallow. Seeing Ty's name on his screen calmed him some. Although he didn't feel like answering, he knew that he had to. He had up and left without saying a word to anyone.

"Hello." He answered.

"Where are you?" Ty asked.

"I'm in the states. I need to handle something."

Ty caught on to the tone in Bleek's voice. Every other word, his voice cracked. Whatever Bleek had to handle, Ty knew that emotions were attached to it.

"What's going on with you bro, talk to me," Ty said.

"Man, I just need to handle some shit." Bleek snapped without meaning to. He was slowly losing his shit, and he knew it. Ty could hear him unraveling.

"Do you need men?" Ty asked calmly.
He had more than enough army to spare for any situation that Bleek could have possibly been in.

"No, bro, this is personal," Bleek said.

"Personal? Do you need me?"

Ty was ready and willing to get on his jet and head back to the states to handle whatever side by side with Bleek. Even after his last trip to the states that could have been deadly, he still was willing to risk it all to help his brother.

Bleek sighed. He didn't want Ty involved at all. Especially knowing that he held harbored feelings for Eternity.

"Bro, no, I have to be the one to handle this. I don't need you coming out of retirement. I'll put you up on game later."
Although Ty didn't want to let the topic go, he did.

"Aight, hit my line if anything. I mean it."

"I got chu."
Bleek ended the line and then sighed. The conversation between him and Tori hours ago played in his head...

"Hello," Bleek answered his phone, annoyed that the same number was interrupting his night.

"Bleek... Bleek, it's Tori. Please get on a plane and come to Tennessee. Eternity needs you."

Instantly his heart sunk. Yet again, he wondered what could have happened in Eternity's life. He knew that it had to be deadly or, if not borderline, for her sister to reach out to him. He heard crying in the background and what sounded like babbling talk.

"Can I speak to her?" he asked.
Something told him that the crying voice in the background belonged to Eternity.

"She can't..." Tori paused and started to whisper, "she can't talk right now. She doesn't know that I called you."

"Okay, okay. I'll be there by tomorrow morning."

"I'll text you the address," Tori said just before she ended the line.

Bleek blinked his eyes when he heard the call for his flight. His phone vibrated in his hand, and yet again, he feared the worst, another call from Tori. When he saw that it was Sha Facetime calling him, he answered.

"*Yo,*" he untangled his headphones and then quickly plugged them into his phone.

"*You bout to get on the plane?*"

"*Yea, I'm boarding now. What it's looking like for you?*" Bleek spoke as he made his way to board the plane.

"*I'm about three hours out.*" Bleek looked down in his phone.

"*What?*" Sha asked, "*I left as soon as you called, bro.*" Bleek chuckled, he was grateful to have a man like Sha in his corner. He was always on go.

A ten-hour trip he was taking with a van full of weaponry. Loyal. So loyal that he didn't care about the risks that came with traveling this way. When Bleek called and told him that he needed him, he was pulling up.

"*My guy…*" Bleek said proudly, "*yo I'm boarding now. Ima hit you when I land aight.*"

"*See you out there, bro. I'll be at the airport for you.*" Sha said before he ended the line.

Bleek walked onto the plane. Not knowing what awaited him made him feel uneasy. *If he beat her ass again, she better really be done for real this time. She got a kid to live for.* He thought as he slowly walked to his first-class seat.

hapter 10

2 days prior…
Chattanooga, TN

"Well, you're getting around better," Tori complimented.

She watched as Eternity made her way around her kitchen.

"Girl, this ain't nothing but the pain killers doing its work," Eternity said with a smile.

The morning sickness lately was getting to Tori, so Eternity came over to make her some breakfast. She held onto her nephew as she watched her sister put cream cheese on the bagel that had just come out of the toaster.

"Stopppp, auntie baby, you can not have my phone," Tori said to the child that was sitting in her lap.
She pulled her phone out of his firm grasp.

"Sis he strong as hell," she said to Eternity.

"He really is. Take him downstairs with Vincent and Man-Man. Me and you need to have a little chat."

Tori raised her eyebrow in suspicion. She didn't know what her sister wanted to talk about, but she was eager to find out.

Without saying a word, she traveled towards the basement, Man-Man's man cave. She walked through the basement and ended her travels in the game room. She knew that's where the two men had to be.

"Special delivery," she said with a smile, interrupting the deep conversation that they were having.

Tori looked at Man-Man and saw that something was wrong by his facial expression. It was evident that he was bothered by whatever conversation he and Vincent were having.

"Ayeee, there go my bwoy. Bring him here TeeBae.'" Vincent put down the gaming controller and then reached his arms out for his son. Tori walked in his direction, still observing Man-Man. In her eyes, she was asking him *what's wrong?* But his facial expression was stone cold. Deciding on leaving him alone about whatever bothered him, she just gave her nephew to Vincent and then made her way back upstairs.

"Tori."

The sound of Man-Man's voice caused her to turn around. Without saying a word, she gave him eye contact to let him know that she was listening.

"The doorbell will ring in a little bit. I'll answer it because it's business… okay."

"Okay."

Tori said and then turned around to make her exit. *Business never comes to this house. What the fuck are they up to?* She wondered.

When she made it back upstairs, Eternity was in the living room with their food. The sight of the meals on the coffee table made her stomach growl.

She rubbed her stomach to calm the hunger and morning sickness. *You're about to eat lil baby,* she thought to herself.

"Come sit, let's chat."

Eternity nodded her head to the other sofa that sat in the room. Both women started to eat in silence.

"So," Eternity paused to chew, "when are you gonna tell me that you're pregnant?"

Tori almost spit the orange juice she was drinking out.

"Wha... what?" Tori questioned.

"Wha... what? Nothing. The proof is everywhere. Do you think I didn't hear you throwing your guts up when we came this morning? Or how about this sweaty look you got to your skin. Or maybe, we should talk about how your nephew is stuck on you. Oh, yea, and I saw your prenatal pills on the kitchen counter before Man-Man came and got them."

Eternity stopped speaking and then just stared at her younger sister. Tori wore a face of shock. She finished the whole glass of orange juice before she decided to plead her case.

"There was so much going on with you. I just didn't want to say anything."

"Pshh," Eternity made the noise with her mouth, "don't ever put one of the happiest moments in your life on the back burner for me. *I'm good.*"

Her last statement was drenched in uncertainty.

"Are you really?" Tori looked over her shoulder to make sure that no one stood in the hall that led to the basement, "did you get the test done for Malik?"

Eternity sighed. She hated discussing this. The results were something that she feared.

"No… not yet."

Tori sucked her teeth.

"And why not?" She asked.

"Two days ago, I called Malik and left a message for him to call me back. Not only did he not call me back, but a woman answered, and later when I went to call back, my number was blocked.

"You play so many games with that man what else did you expect. You think he's supposed to wait around for you. Why did you even call him without getting the test done yet?" Tori questioned.

"Because I know that he will have us despite the results."

Tori opened her eyes widely and then looked over her shoulder. When she saw that the coast was clear, she spoke.

"Have y'all? Are you thinking about leaving? For good this time?"

Eternity shook her head up and down.

"Yes," she confirmed.

"But things with you and Vee seem to be—"

"They aren't. Nothing about him and I are good. We're not fighting or anything, but the love ain't there for real. It hadn't been since I came home from the hospital. He's an amazing father to Malik. It's just... I don't know. I just feel like I'm more in love with the memories that I shared with him. That's how I know. My love for him just isn't there anymore," Eternity confessed.

Tori wasn't even given a chance to respond because the doorbell went off before she could open her mouth.

Ding, Ding

Ding, Ding

"You just gone sit there like you don't hear your bell ringing?" Eternity asked.

"Yep."

"I'm coming!"

Both ladies turned their attention to Man-Man, who had just walked past and headed to the front door.

"It took you too long to come to the door, Marcelo."

Tori almost broke her neck as she turned around to see who the woman was in her home.

"Who is that?" Eternity whispered.

"I don't know, Marcelo said it was *business*."

"Business? And she's calling him by his government?"

Tori didn't have a response for her sister because she didn't know much. That bothered her. Man-Man started to walk past the two ladies in the living room. Tori and Eternity's eyes locked on the woman that trailed behind him. She wore a short mink coat and some waxed jeans paired with some designer booties. Her light skin was blemish-free, and her pink lips held a tint of gloss. Her eyes were narrowed, and her face was emotionless. She looked like nothing to play with.

"Oooo, she looks really boujee," Eternity said in a snobbish tone.

"Yea, she does…"

Tori was too trapped in her own thoughts to joke with her sister. *Who the fuck is that bitch?* She wondered. When it came to *the business* that Man-Man was talking about, she was sure that she had formally met everyone. She knew everyone from the dealers, to the runners, to the testers. *She has to be a new worker.* She quickly concluded in her head.

"You brought him back upstairs so y'all can handle y'all little business?" Eternity's voice broke Tori from her thoughts. Tori looked up and saw that Man-Man was joining them with her nephew in tow.

"Vee is the one that has business to handle. Ima kick it here with y'all." He said to Eternity before he directed his attention to Tori. "I don't even know why he had to handle business here. I'm sorry bae that *she's* here."

Tori looked his way and then gave him a slight smile.

"What are you apologizing for? If he has to handle business with a *worker* than so be it. I just didn't expect it to be a woman."

"Oh, she's not a worker, she's the plug, and I'm apologizing because she's also my ex-wife."

The smile on Tori's face quickly faded. Eternity looked between the couple and then smacked her lips together. She didn't have any words to share.

"Nova Lee, what's up with ya? Have a seat."

Vincent patted the spot on the couch next to him.

"For one, don't call me that. That name is reserved for my sisters and my sisters only." She took off her coat and then draped it over her forearm.

Instead of taking the seat beside him, she took place on the chair across from him.

"I thought he would have gotten rid of these chairs here," she rubbed the arms of the chair she sat in.

"Come on now, Nova. You reached out and said you got that info for me. You could have told me over the phone who the man is mayne."

"I couldn't have. You have no idea who you have stumbled across."

Vincent rubbed his beard and then sat back into his chair.

"Well, we could have met anywhere. Now, why did you jump at the opportunity to meet here and only here, Ms. Nova?"

A smirked formed on her face. Making her already slanted eyes slant more.

"Oh, no reason."

She's so full of games. Vincent thought as he shook his head.

"So, tell me about this dude."

Nova crossed one leg over the other and then sighed. She didn't know what mess Vincent had gotten himself into, but she knew that raging on a war with a Ruiz Dynasty affiliate could be deadly. The last thing that she wanted to do was to lose a good worker. Over the years, Vincent had made her and her sisters very wealthy.

"Well, for starters. He's from Brooklyn, New York. A few years ago, he was wanted for murder, but that case was dismissed due to a lack of evidence. He's a Ruiz Dynasty affiliate."

"What is a nigga doing with Spanish ties?" Vincent interrupted.

Every hood hustler had heard about the Ruiz Dynasty.

"I have no clue, but he's rooted deep within that organization too. I'm talking top five on the totem pole. If my intel is right, then he is up there with Julian himself. He's directly under Tyshawn Barnett."

Fuck, Vincent thought to himself. All of the stories he had heard of the Ruiz Dynasty started to plague his mind. Still, he wondered what the man in the pictures had to do with Eternity. Besides them both being from Brooklyn, he didn't see a comparison.

"I just don't see what this dude has to do with my lady," he openly admitted.

"Well, I don't have the answers to that. The only thing that I can do is warn you. If you're trying to go to the source for answers, then proceed with caution. Malik Browne is not to be underestimated."

Vincent's eyes shot open. Now his interest was peaked.

"Say his name again."

"Malik Browne," Nova answered casually.

Vincent ran his hand down the side of his face. Hearing that the name of his son was the same name as the mystery man had him tripping. He wanted to name their boy Andre, but Eternity insisted on the name Malik. So, lost in his thoughts, he couldn't hear Nova speaking to him.

"Walk me out through the back, please," she ordered.

Vincent shook his head to push his thoughts to the back of his mind.

"Why the back?" He asked.

"Because I already had all eyes on me during the walk-in. It makes no sense to make them sweat twice."

She stood and then put on her coat.

"That's why you brought ya ass over here. You wanted to be known, huh?"

She chuckled.

"Your words, not mine."

She said as she followed him out the back.

After standing in the garage and holding small talk with Nova before she was driven off by her chauffeur, Vincent entered the house through the front.

"Once again... you can NOT just say that she's your ex-wife so fucking nonchalantly."
Vincent walked into the living room to find Tori standing over Man-Man while he sat on the sofa. As she spoke, she had her fingers pointed in his face.

"We were having this conversation like humans. Now you want to yell, and you know I'm not with that shit."
Man-Man's voice was steady. It came off as unbothered, but Vincent knew that's just how he was. Never did he get too overly excited about anything.

Eternity made brief eye contact with him, and then she turned her attention back to the show in the room. Vincent's eyes rolled down to the baby she had seated in her lap. He shook the rattle in his hand, every once in a while, putting it in his mouth and then taking it out.

"Big baby, let's go. Let's leave em to talk."
The sound of Vincent's voice caused Tori to turn around. She had a bone to pick with him as well.

"And your bald-headed ass thought it would be a magnificent idea if y'all handled business here in MY home?"

Man-Man smirked at how she took ownership of their home. For months she expressed wanting to buy their own home and move after the baby was born. She didn't want to raise her child in a house that he had shared with his ex-wife.

Eternity lightly chuckled because her little sister was the mirror image of her. When she had arguments with Vincent, she would be the first to call him bald-headed.

"TeeBae, the information that I needed was very important. She said she was only giving it to me if we met here."
Tori paced the floors in front of everyone.

"Oh, so she's a manipulative bitch that wants to get seen?" She said out loud although she was more so talking to herself. She turned her attention back towards Man-Man.

"I better not ever cross paths with her again. I'll beat her the fuck up, and that's on my momma."

She walked over to Eternity and then showered her nephew with kisses before she stormed out of the living room. She made sure to bump Vincent during her exit.

"Her little ass is a firecracker, ain't she?" Vincent asked as he shook off the bump, she had given him.

"Let's go, big baby. Let's head on home."
He walked over and then got the baby out her lap so that she could get herself together.

Carefully he studied the child in his arms. He focused on every feature. He zoned in on every little detail in the child in his arms. He tried to find similarities.

"I'm ready," Eternity said, breaking him from his daze.

"Aight cool. Later bwoy," Vincent said to Man-Man as he and Eternity walked out. Man-Man ignored Vincent because he was still pissed at the situation that he was put in. *All of this drama just to get some street intel,* Man-Man thought to himself as he watched Vincent close the door to his home.

Chapter 11

The entire ride home Vincent couldn't help but think about the coincidence of the man from the pictures having the same name as his son. When they made it home, he helped Eternity into the bed. She wasn't one hundred percent back to normal, so he knew that the pressure she applied to her ankle during the simple task of walking had to have had her exhausted.

"Get you some rest ima go out and get us something for lunch and dinner. I'm taking Malik with me, so rest up." Vincent watched as Eternity smiled brightly. Her having time to herself was rare these days. Vincent went to use the bathroom before he did his runarounds. When he came back into the room, he reached out his arms, when their baby lifted his arms to be picked up, Vincent scooped him into his arms.

"Say we'll be back, Mommy." Vincent said in a baby voice as he used Malik's tiny hand to wave goodbye.

After putting the baby's coat back on, he headed out the door. His travels ended at an Any Lab Test Now facility that was located on Lee Highway.

"Hello sir, how may I help you?"

Vincent was asked as soon as he walked in the door. He adjusted the baby bag onto his shoulder and then held onto Malik a little bit tighter before he responded.

"I need to get this baby tested. I need to know if I'm the father."
His tone was low like he didn't want the other people waiting to hear him.

"Okay, we can do that for you. Will the mother be joining us?" The woman behind the desk asked.

"No."

"Although we don't need it, it might make results quicker. Do you have a sample from the mother?"

Vincent pulled a zip lock bag out of the diaper bag that hung from his shoulder.

"Is this okay for the sample?" He asked.

"Yes, this is fine." The woman responded as she took the zip lock bag from Vincent.

"You can come around to the back," she said as she buzzed the door for him.

Once, she collected all of the information that she needed from him. She swabbed his mouth and then Malik's mouth.

"Come on, bwoy, don't start this crying," Vincent said when the baby in his lap started to whimper.

"How soon can I get the results back?" Vincent asked as he prepared himself to leave.

"Three to five business days."

"Three to five, what? Nawl mam, I need these back as soon as possible. Christmas is a few days away, so I know y'all gone be closed. Please mam… anything sooner will do."

The woman stopped walking out of the room. Looking at the desperation in Vincent's eyes, she quickly found an alternative for him.

"Well, the results can be ready tomorrow, but that will cost extra."

"I'm fine with that. What time do I come tomorrow to get it?"

"We close at five, so anytime before then."

Vincent thanked the woman and then made his exit. The entire ride to get food, he was distracted. After getting the food the rest of the ride home, he was so into his thoughts that it took him a while to even notice that the baby in the back seat was crying.

He looked at the time on his dashboard and then shook his head. It was Malik's feeding time.

"Aight my bwoy we almost home then you can eat, okay?" He reached his right arm towards the backseat. With his hand dangling over the car seat, Malik reached up and grabbed his hand. Soon, his crying seized to exist. Since he was a newborn, he hated car rides that weren't filled with talk. If he didn't hear voices, he would cry.

Vincent learned that just with his hand being held that Malik would be calm enough to sleep. *He gotta be mine. Nobody knows this shit about him. H*e thought as he rubbed the back of Malik's tiny hand. Tears came to his eyes at the thought of Malik not being his. Briefly, he took his hand off of the wheel and then wiped the tears that started to stain his cheeks. He wouldn't dare take his hand from Malik to wipe his face. He would always put his children's needs above his own.

He knew that the brief second he would use to take his hand from Malik would cause the child discomfort. He wouldn't dare.

"I gotta be his dad," he whimpered to himself.

His grip around the steering wheel tightened at the thought of him not being. He held the steering wheel so tightly that his callused fingertips started to turn white. Rage began to build in his soul at the possibility of him not being. He breathed in and out to control his thoughts. Deep breaths. He had to control himself.

In rehab, he learned how vital mediation before action was. As he pulled into his driveway, he drilled in his head the importance of self-control. Still not wanting to show his hand until test results were in his grasp, he had to wear this mask around Eternity. After gathering the bags and the baby, he walked into the house.

90's music lightly played in his home. It was a tell-tale sign that Eternity was in a great mood. Either that or it was cleaning day. Knowing that he hired a cleaning service to keep the house intact over the past few months because of her injury, he knew that the sweet sounds of Escape had to because of her mood. He placed the food bags on the kitchen island and then undressed the baby before he climbed the stairs with him in tow. When he pushed his room door open, the music only intensified.

There's no way that we can work it out
If we don't pull together
I don't mean to be demanding
I want some understanding
I wanna be with you
What I need from you is understanding
How can we communicate
If you don't hear what I say
What I need from you is understanding
So simple as 1, 2,3
Understanding is what I need

He saw that the room was empty and that the bathroom door was slightly open. The sweet sound of Eternity singing along could be lowly heard. She could always hold a note, although she hated to admit it. Being so used to noise being the center of the household, Malik was still sleep in Vincent's arms. Gently, the baby was placed into the bassinet that stood in the corner of the room.

Like how Sirens used to lure sailors with their melody to rocks in the sea, Eternity's sweet voice was pulling him towards their bathroom. He pushed open the door and then just watched her. She stood in the mirror, wrapped in a towel flat ironing her hair. He could tell that she had washed it because one end was shrunken in size while the other side that was pressed touched the middle of her back. She stopped singing when she saw him through the mirror. Slightly, she smiled.

She thought of where they stood while they made eye contact. He was a good man, now at least. The man she had prayed for every single night before bed he had finally become. Yet, he was no longer for her. She no longer felt what she used to, but still, she loved him. Now that she was serious with the thought of leaving, he seemed to be perfect. So perfect.

"You got panties on under there?" He asked lowly as he slowly took steps towards her.
Without uttering a word, she shook her head from left to right.

"Mmm," he grumbled as he took his strong hands and then traced them up to her thighs.

His hands went under her towel and cupped her juicy rear end. For the first time in a long time, he became erect. He was ready to part her middle right where they stood.

"Where's Malik?"

Eternity questioned the whereabouts of her child. Vincent silently cringed at her question. The only thing he could think about was what Nova had told him about Malik Browne. Vincent closed his eyes tightly to shut out the thought of this other man. All he wanted to do was enjoy the moment with Eternity. He didn't know how the next day would go for him, but he did know that Malik Browne was a dead ass regardless of the test results.

"He's sleeping, but he gone be up any minute. Am I good on this quickie?"

He asked as he rubbed her frame with one hand while he dropped his jeans and drawers with the other. Before she could finish shaking her head up and down to agree with him, he bent her over the sink and then pushed into her garden.

"Shitttt you tight as fuck," he hissed as he stroked in and out of her honey pot.

"Ouchhhh."

Vincent stopped and then looked in the mirror at her facial expression. Her face was comforted into pain. He pulled out of her and then turned her around.

Picking her up, he placed her onto the bathroom counter. The position he just had her in was putting weight on her injured ankle, and he knew it. As soon as she was placed onto the countertop, she parted her legs. He hovered over her with his bottom lip pulled in between his teeth. Ready to go to work. Ready to release all pain he had within him. The burden he was carrying on the question of this paternity was killing him. He had to release.

Eternity wrapped her arms around the back of his neck as he rocked her boat. She closed her eyes tightly and enjoyed the moment because it felt final. Gushing noises broke her from her thoughts.

"You hear that bae? You opening up for ya bwoy. Come on and bust one."

Vincent whispered in her ear as he kept the same pace. His arms wrapped around her as he worked her middle. The sound of crying started as soon as they both hit their climax. Vincent helped Eternity down from the counter, quickly cleaned himself up at the sink, and then went to tend to the crying baby.

Too exhausted to finish her hair, Eternity figured that she would just do it the next day. She blew out a sharp breath at the pain from her ankle. She held onto the bathroom counter to brace herself. She snatched her pill bottle off the counter and then opened it. After pouring one tablet into the palm of her hand, she put the bottle back.

She ran the water in the sink, popped the pill into her mouth, and then put her lips under the faucet. When enough water was gathered in her mouth to take the pill easily, she swallowed. She slowly limped over to the shower, turned on the water, and then quickly rewashed. When she exited the bathroom, she saw that Vincent was feeding Malik and that there was a food bag on her nightstand.

Quickly she dressed in pajamas and then took a seat next to them.

"Did you eat already?" She asked Vincent.

"Na, not yet. He about to finish this bottle and ima put him down for the night."

Eternity smiled as she briefly watched his interaction with the baby. Although he was no longer considered a newborn, Vincent still handled him with care. When he finished feeding the child, he walked him down to his nursery.

Eternity started to dig into the food containers when Vincent made his exit. Shortly he returned and then took a seat next to her. Together they ate silently.

"Tomorrow, go out. Call TeeBae or something. Ima take Malik with me since it's my day with my other kids."

Vincent said, breaking the awkward silence. His kids were on Christmas break, so his daughter that lived in Atlanta was in town. After the strain she had put on her ankle, he knew that she would need a day of pampering. Eternity didn't give a response; instead, she reached her hand out for his food tray.

"I'll take the garbage downstairs." She offered. Vincent quickly rose from the bed.

"Na bae, you rest that damn ankle. I'll take the garbage out."

Vincent held his hand out for her tray, so she placed the container into his hand. He grabbed his own box and then put it inside of the plastic bag that the food had come in. When he made it downstairs, he pulled the garbage from the kitchen can and then headed out the front door. The next day the garbage men would be coming around, so he dragged the big green garbage cans to the curb for them.

He walked back into the house, washed his hands at the kitchen sink, and then made his way back up to his bedroom. When he entered the room, he saw that Eternity was asleep. The only time she would fall asleep that fast is when she actually took the pain killers that the doctor had prescribed for her.

Vincent decided to wash his body before he got into the bed. After quickly taking care of his hygiene, he crawled into the bed beside Eternity. For hours he stared at the dark ceiling. Slight rays from the moon's light that peeked through the blinds gave the room a little light, but for the most part, the entire room was pitch black. So troubled, he tossed and turned to try and find comfort. It wasn't until Eternity unknowingly laid her head on his chest that he found his comfortable spot. Finally, he closed his eyes and drifted off to sleep.

*CC*hapter 12

Eternity woke in the morning to an empty house. At Vincent's request, she was going to take the day to enjoy herself. She had called Tori and told her that the day was theirs to enjoy. Tori had the perfect place for them to go and agreed to come by to pick Eternity up. So, Eternity knew that she had limited time to get ready. Being child-free, she felt like she could breathe a little. It was such a refreshing feeling, not having to worry about changing diapers or making bottles. Even if it was only for a few hours, she was grateful for the time she was given.

She looked at her cane that was propped up against her room wall and sucked her teeth. The temporary assist that she was given to aide her with outside activities was cramping her style. She decided on just wearing her medical boot for the day.

She made sure to grab socks that matched her outfit since one of them would be showing. She made her way to her bathroom to brush her teeth and wash her face. Standing in front of the sink, she looked for her toothbrush. Being that she was spending so much time at Tori's house, she figured that she had left it over there. She reached under her sink to grab a fresh toothbrush from a new pack and then brushed her teeth so that she could start her day.

After flat ironing the other side of her head that she didn't tend to the day before she got dressed. It took her longer than expected to get ready. She struggled down the stairs. Even with her taking a break in the middle, still, she worked up quite the sweat.

When she got to the bottom of the steps, she used the back of her hand to wipe the perspire from her forehead. She heard keys in her door as she limped over to her closet. She thought that Vincent had forgotten something. Instead, Tori walked through the door and then went to turn the alarm system off. Since Eternity had gotten hurt, she had started putting her spare key back to use. The last thing that she wanted was her sister rushing to the door and then getting more hurt in the process.

"You ready to go?" Tori asked.

"Yea, I'm getting my jacket now. Where are we going again?"

Eternity knew that the day was hers, but she just didn't know how she would be spending it.

"We're gonna go to the spa. I want to put these Christmas coupons to use. They are closed tomorrow for Christmas Eve, and they are closed Christmas Day. So, we have to go today."
Eternity looked at her sister as she talked, and finally, she was starting to see the pregnancy weight on her. Her cheeks were fuller, and her skin looked radiant.

"What?" Tori asked when she noticed that her sister was staring.

"Nothing, ToriTee. Pregnancy just looks good on you." Eternity said with a smile, "your baby bump is starting to peek," she added.

"Man, save all that mushy stuff, and let's go."
Tori led the way outside, and Eternity slowly followed.

While Tori got the car started, Eternity limped over to her mailbox. She opened it, and then her heart began to beat rapidly when an envelope caught her attention. She had been waiting on this exact piece of mail. She quickly ripped it open and then skimmed over the documents. Her eyes watered once she found what she was looking for.

"Ughhh," she groaned as she stuffed the paperwork into her purse.

"Don't walk back up the driveway I'ma back out!" Tori yelled out of the car window.
Eternity shook her head and then waited on her sister. Now, more than ever, she needed the day of pampering.

The two women sat in the pedicure chairs.

"Mmmm, this feels so good," Tori groaned as the back massager in the chair pressed against her spine. Stepping into her second trimester, she had started to experience more back pains than a little. Eternity was skeptical about getting a pedicure. Her cuts on her ankle were healed, but still, the skin was very sensitive to the touch.

"I need you to be very careful with this foot here," Eternity said to the nail technician as she pointed to her left foot.

"Sis," she said in her sweetest tone as she looked over at Tori.

Tori was too busy enjoying her back massage. Her eyes were closed, and her head was rested against the headrest.

"ToriTee."

Tori shot her eyes open, "huh?" she asked Eternity.

"Look, I know tomorrow is Christmas Eve, but I was wondering if you could watch Malik for a few hours. I really want to talk to Vincent about me leaving tomorrow.'"

Tori opened her mouth slightly from the shock. *She's really serious about leaving.* She thought before she responded.

"I'll take him tonight and bring him back home tomorrow," she said, "so you really trynna leave, huh?" She asked.

Eternity sighed. It was something she was thinking of long and hard. The night before was a sign in her head, the goodbye sex. It had to be. It was too intimate, too romantically perfect. In her mind, it had to be a sign from God that the end was near. Without speaking to Bleek, she didn't know where she was headed, but she knew that the relationship she had with Vincent had passed.

"Yea, I'm serious about leaving," she confirmed, "even if for whatever reason me and Bleek don't happen, he still has that store for me. I can turn that into something great I don't know what yet, but it can be something."

Tori listened to her sister talk. Hearing how she had every detail covered, she knew that her sister was serious.

"Well, you know I got your back."

And just like that, the conversation between the two of them was finished. Tori felt sad knowing that for the rest of her pregnancy that her sister wouldn't be present, but she had no intention of voicing that opinion. She wore a smile on her face as she and her sister made small talk. For once, Eternity was putting her needs first, and Tori wasn't going to stand in the way of that. For as long as she could remember, Tori saw that her sister put everyone else's needs above her own. Tori knew that her sister had a good heart because even when she tried to put herself first, she ended up feeling bad for it.

After spending hours in the spa, Tori and Eternity were driving back to Eternity's house.

"I wanna stop for some Mc Donald's really quick." Tori said as she rubbed her stomach.

"Whatever my niece or nephew wants give it to them." Eternity reached over and then gently rubbed Tori's growing baby bump. Tori pulled into the drive-thru and then got what her stomach was craving.

"You really didn't want anything, sis?" Tori asked as she bit a handful of fries in one hand and then controlled the steering wheel with the other.

"Na sis, I got some shrimp alfredo inside that I have a taste for."

Eternity leaned back in her seat and enjoyed the rest of the ride to her home. Being that they were only at the Mc Donald's, that was around the corner; the trip was short. When Eternity didn't see Vincent's car in the driveway, she assumed that he was still out with the kids. Her and Tori exited the vehicle and then made their way inside.

Although Eternity had a day of relaxation still, she was drained. Things that she took for granted before like the simple task of walking had her winded now of days. After they walked through the door, they were greeted with a beeping noise. Slowly Eternity made her way to the alarm system on the wall. When she read the screen that said: Ready to alarm, she tilted her head to the side.

Many times before, Vincent would rush out of the house and forget to turn the alarm on. She took off her coat and then hung it in the hallway closet as she rolled her eyes at his lack for their safety. Vincent was the kind of man that was cocky when it came to his street cred. In his mind, no one walking the earth had the balls to come for him because of the status quo that he had built for himself.

Tori walked to the living room with her Mc Donald's bag and then took a seat on the couch. The only reason why she was hanging around is that she was waiting for Vincent to return with her nephew. Although she was tired, she was going to keep her word with her sister.

"Sis, did you turn the alarm off?" Tori asked.
The beeping noise was still going off from when they had walked in.

"It wasn't even the alarm system, so it has to be the answering machine." Eternity said as she limped into the living room.

She made her way over to the end table that held her house phone, and then she sat in the chair next to the table. Her ankle was killing her. All-day, she went without taking her prescribed pain killers because they made her drowsy. Now she was paying the price for not aiding herself with the drugs earlier in the day. She picked up her foot with the boot on it and then placed it onto the coffee table that stood in front of her. She reached down and then unstrapped the medical boot on her foot.

Tori's phone started to ring and then she smiled when she saw that it was Man-Man calling her. She quickly answered her phone as Eternity pressed the play button on the answering machine to the house phone.

"Uhhhh, I just find it funny how you can't seem to answer your phone V-dub."
Eternity rolled her eyes at the sound Treasure's voice.

"Anyway… how the hell you ask for your son today, but you don't come and get him? You have a new kid and just forget about ya others, huh? Call me back when you get this. You have a lot of explaining to do."

Eternity leaned her body to the side so that she could get her cellphone that was in her back pocket. She called Vincent on her phone, but it rang and then went straight to voicemail. She picked the house phone up from the receiver and then called him from that, but again the call went straight to voicemail. In an instant, her stomach went hallow. Something in her gut was telling her that something was wrong. She thought of the safety of her child first. Seconds later, the safety of Vincent crossed her mind.

She stood to her feet. She had to hold onto the arm of the chair to balance herself because the pain that radiated from her ankle to her calf was unbearable.

"Whoa bae lemme call you right back," Tori said into her phone before she hung up. She turned her attention to Eternity, "sis what's wrong?" she asked.

"Something isn't right…" Eternity mumbled lowly. Still, Tori heard what she had said.

Eternity made her way towards Vincent's office. She had to replay the cameras from outside to see when the last time Vincent was in the house. Not knowing what could have happened to him or her son had her stomach in knots. While Eternity slowly made her way to the office, Tori had replayed the message on the answering machine. She had missed it the first time because of her phone call.

When Eternity walked into Vincent's office, she saw that it was a mess. His chair that sat behind his desk was turned over, and his safe was wide open.

"Tori! Tori, we got robbed!" She yelled out as she rushed over to the safe.

"Y'all got what?" Tori ran into the office and found Eternity standing in front of the safe with a paper in her hand. Eternity's hand was up against the wall to give her support because she felt like her knees were about to give out from under her.

"What's wrong, sis?" Tori asked.

Eternity's eyes watered as she reread the letter.

ONE MALIK FOR THE OTHER. THE CHOICE IS YOURS.

At the bottom of the page, three small images of her and Bleek when they were at Mr. T's a few months ago were plastered. Although the pictures were little, she could see them clearly.

"Oh my God, he has my baby!" she cried out.

"What?" Tori asked in a confused state. She walked over to Eternity and then snatched the paper out of her sister's hand.

"How did he? How the fuck? What am I?" Eternity choked over her words as she held onto her chest. She leaned on the desk in the room to hold her up.

"What is this a fucking game or something?" Tori asked as she carefully examined the paper in her hand. Both women wondered how the pictures were even taken, but their main concern went to the missing baby.

Loudly, Eternity cried. She couldn't compose herself. She didn't know how much Vincent knew, but she knew that he knew enough to run off with her child.

"What am I supposed to do?"

"Just umm… we are going to figure this out. Just give me a minute; maybe Marcello knows where he is."
Tori said before she quickly exited the room. She walked back into the living room and then picked her cellphone up from the couch.

Quickly her mind began to run with thoughts. The last thing that she wanted to do was to involve her man in this. Judging by the note and the pictures at the bottom of the picture, she knew that Vincent had to be unraveling by the second. The child in her stomach gave her butterflies. There was no way that she was about to put her child's father into the line of fire. Her own stomach felt hollow at the thought of anything happening to her man.

That feeling faded when the heart-wrenching feeling of anything happening to her nephew took over. Her sister had been through so much. She knew that she couldn't bear heartache or pain anymore. Tori had half a mind to call the police, but she knew, just like everyone else in Chattanooga, that Vincent had the local officers on payroll. Calling Man-Man would result in him driving around trying to find Vincent, and she knew that while Vincent was in his current state that it was too dangerous. Still, she knew that she had to bring Man-Man into the light with this current situation.

"What happens if he hurts my baby?" she heard Eternity yell out from the back room.

It was evident that she was still crying by the way her voice cracked with each word. *Come on, come on answer.* Tori thought to herself as the phone rung in her ear. After ringing out, the phone number she was calling went to voicemail. She called right back.

"Hello." The man answered on the second ring.

"Bleek... Bleek, it's Tori. Please get on a plane and come to Tennessee. Eternity needs you." Tori said quickly. Her nerves were so bad that she was stuttering over her words.

In the background, Eternity started crying louder.

"My fucking heart! I cannah," the rest of her words were babbled talk.

"Can I speak to her?" Bleek asked.

Tori closed her eyes to catch a grip. Hearing her sister cry like that had tears coming to her own eyes.

"She can't..." Tori paused and started to whisper, *"she can't talk right now. She doesn't know that I called you."*

"Okay, okay. I'll be there by tomorrow morning."

"I'll text you the address," Tori said just before she ended the line.

She quickly went to her text messages and then sent Bleek the address to her home. She knew that there was no way that she and Eternity could stay where they were. Not when the walls surrounding them were a constant reminder of her nephew. She knew that no location would ease Eternity's worries, but at least at her home, it was different surroundings.

The thought of bringing her sister to her homemade her quickly think of Man-Man.

"Fuck, I gotta tell him too." She mumbled to herself. Her pregnancy had caused her to get sidetracked at times quickly. Eternity had gotten too quiet. Quickly Tori ran to the office in the back to find Eternity in the same spot she had left her. Only now, she stood with her arms wrapped around her body. Slowly she rocked back and forth as she held herself. She was staring at a spot on the wall. She was lost in oblivion.

Snot covered her upper lip, but she didn't dare wipe it. Tori called Man-Man on her phone. She knew that she wouldn't be able to get Eternity to leave the house on her own.

"Hello?" he answered on the first ring.

"Drop what you're doing and come to Eternity's house. Now." Tori blurted out everything without even taking a breath.

"I'm on my way. What happened?"

"Your cousin is missing with Malik. There's so much to explain. Just get here, please."

"Okay."

Man-Man hung up the phone. Tori went to Eternity and then hugged her. Her older sister crumbled in her embrace.

"I was literally leaving today. I was one foot out of the door." She cried onto Tori's shoulder.

"Shh, shhh. Marcelo is on his way over here, and then we are going to go to my house. We will get to the bottom of this sis." Tori assured as she rubbed her sister's back.

Chapter 13

Present Day
Chattanooga, TN

"How was the drive?" Bleek asked Sha as he got into the passenger side of the work van.

Sha rolled his neck in a circular motion to get the cramp out.

"It wasn't that bad for real. I'm just happy to be here. We handle what we gotta handle, stash all this shit at the shop, and then I can fly my ass home, word."

Bleek held his hand out for a dap, and then they embraced in a gangster's handshake.

"Thank you for coming boy, I appreciate it."

"Always bro always," Sha responded before driving away from the airport.

The ride to the address that Tori had given Bleek was a silent one. Bleek was so wrapped in his own thoughts while Sha was just down for the ride. The dynamic duo of silence. Silent killers that were ready to murk something, anything.

"Turn right onto Oriole Drive, and then your destination is on the right."

The navigation broke their silence. Sha made the right onto the block. They drove past houses with grassed yards and driveways attached.

"*Arrived.*"

The navigation said, which caused Sha to pull over to the house that was on the right of them.

"Sit here for a minute let me go see what's going on," Bleek said as he unbuckled his seat belt.

"Na bro. I'm coming with you this shit could be—"

"It's not. This is my sister's house."

"Aight, well, I'll be right here then," Sha said as he took off his seat belt and then leaned his chair back.

Bleek got out of the car and then closed the door behind him. He stretched to knock off the tension in his body from the drive over. He sighed and then ran his hand down the long side of his face. Ending his travels at his beard, he sighed again and then made his way up the walkway. He spotted a red Mercedes Benz and a G wagon in the driveway. *Somebody's living good.* He thought to himself as he eyed the vehicles. Before he could ring the doorbell, the front door swung open.

"I saw you walking up the driveway on the camera."
Bleek looked down at Tori and saw her tear-stained face. She leaned into him for a hug. He opened his arms to hold her.

He took notice of the slight baby bump that poked out in the front of her. While hugging her back, he made sure not to embrace her too hard. He could tell that she was crying by the way her back was heaving up in down in his arms. Her head was rested on his chest while he rubbed her back soothingly.

"Bleek, right?"

Bleek looked up and saw that a man was standing inside the house with his sights fixated on him.

Slowly he pulled away from Tori.

"Who's askin—"

Before Bleek could finish his statement, Tori interrupted.

"Bleek, this is Man-Man. He's my boyfriend."

She stepped out of the way to let Bleek in.

"You can tell your friend in the car that he is welcome to come in," she added as she looked at the van parked out front.

"I'll go get him in a minute," Bleek said as he walked into the house.

He walked over to Man-Man and then held his hand out for a pound. Man-Man took his hand, and then they quickly embraced. Bleek canted his body to the side so that he could speak to Tori. Not wanting to turn his back on Man-Man because he didn't know him, he still managed to give Tori his attention before he spoke.

"Where is she?" he asked.

Tori nodded her head to a hall and then walked past him to lead the way. They walked past the kitchen and into a hall. After passing two doors, Tori opened the third. She nodded into the room and then walked away. Bleek took a deep breath before he entered the room. Slowly he closed the door behind him.

Eternity was lying on the bed in the bedroom with her back facing him. When he heard her sniffles, he froze in place. Then is when he realized that he had traveled almost eight hundred miles and still did not know what was going on. Tori didn't say much on the phone. All he knew is that he was needed. That was all he had to hear to make him detour his travels to her state. To her new home. He would do anything for her.

"How are you here?" she cried out.

He didn't give a verbal response.

"Malik... I know it's you I can smell you." She said.

She would pick up on his Tom Ford cologne anywhere. Like a shark smelling blood in the water, her nose was on him.

He circled around the bed so that she could look directly at her. Something told him that she would have bruises all over her face. That had to be the reason why his presence was needed. When he rounded the bed, they made eye contact. Her eyes were so red, and the space around her sockets was puffy. He could tell that she had been crying for hours. She bit her bottom lip as she smelled his scent, and her body started to tremble.

"Howwww are you hereeeee?" she cried out.

He quickly kicked off his sneakers and then made his way to the bed. He observed her entire body and then noticed the brace that covered one of her ankles. Silently he began to fume. *I knew she would be getting her ass beat again if she fucking stayed,* he thought as he gently climbed over her. He wouldn't dare speak his thoughts because he wasn't the kind of man that was into the: *I told you so.*

Eternity felt Bleek wrap his arm around her from behind. She whimpered as he tried to tend to her.

"I'm no longer asking anymore. You are coming back with me," he said in a stern voice before he sighed and then nestled his face into the crook of her neck.

She smelled tart, but he didn't care. That natural vanilla scent that she always held was underneath the smell of sweat.

"Why is this happening to me? Why is he doing this?" she asked, not to anyone in particular, but Bleek was damn sure going to answer.

"I promise... he will no longer beat your ass. He ain't gone be able to do shit from where I'ma send him. Come on, ma," he paused and then kissed the nape of her neck, "get dressed, round up little man, and let's go."

"I can't go anywhere. He has my son."

"What?" Bleek lifted his body from the bed and then stared down at her.

She contorted her face into so much pain. If Bleek wasn't looking down directly at her, he wouldn't have even known that she was crying.

"He... has... my... son."

Bleek saw her lips moving, but what she said was barely audible.

"Since when?" Bleek said as he got up from the bed immediately.

"Since yesterday and I can't call the police. He... he... he's well connected."

"I'm fucking well connected... he's just a bitch!"
Bleek spoke louder than he intended to, so he lowered his tone. He stood at the foot of the bed and paced for a while before he decided to say anything. Bleek thought of the status that he was just given — the official leader of the Ruiz Dynasty. Not yet knowing the status of his pull, he decided that going down that road was the last resort.

If he wanted, he could have an entire Dominican Army behind him for the war that he was about to fight, but he knew that he could handle things on his own. He had been handling clean up jobs since a teen, so in his mind, getting rid of Vincent wasn't going to be shit but another sweep under the rug. Another hash mark added to his uniform. For years he had been putting in work and although within the last year he played the back and let Sha take the lead, he knew that it was time for him to get his own hands dirty again. This thing with Vincent to him was personal. Anything involving Eternity Washington was personal to him.

"I just don't know what to do. He's missing and only left this behind."

Eternity said as she opened her hand. Bleek didn't notice that she was holding onto a piece of paper until now. Weakly, she held her arm up to hand him the piece of paper. Bleek took the piece of paper out of her hand and then examined it. Instantly, he grew angry. He ran his tongue along inside of his jawline and then bit his bottom lip. Blood slowly trickled into his mouth. He looked down at the pictures of him and Eternity from the pizza shop a few months ago.

His eyes quickly scanned the paper in front of him. Bold letters caught his eye:

ONE MALIK FOR THE OTHER. THE CHOICE IS YOURS.

Quickly Bleek crumbled the paper and then pulled his cellphone out of his coat pocket. With two rings, the noise in his ear ended.

"Yo," Sha answered.

"Come to the front door. This shit is more serious than I thought."

Without saying another word, Bleek ended the line. He then walked to the room door and opened it.

"Tori… get ready to open the door." He called out into the hall.

Shortly after, the doorbell rang.

"Make sure he good I'ma be out in a min, aight?" he added just before he closed the door.

He didn't even wait for a response because he knew that she had to still be in the living room. When he heard mumbled voices talking on the other side of the door, he knew that Sha had made it inside.

He was fuming as he made his way back to Eternity. *What kind of weak muthafucka kidnaps his own kid over some shit like this?* He wondered. The pictures weren't even intimate. He couldn't understand Vincent's motive.

"Give me his number."

Bleek said to Eternity.

Slowly she finally sat up in the bed. The room was spinning as she tried to gather her head.

"I've been calling, and he hasn't been answering."

"I didn't ask you that I said give me his number."

Bleek was slowly losing patience. He had no love for niggas like Vincent, and when he finally caught up to him, he knew exactly what he was going to do to him.

A quick death would be too easy. Torture was the only thing on Bleek's mind, and it was all in the name of Eternity. He would manually pull the eyelids off a man if he used the wrong words with her. The dangers of a man actually hurting her would be ten times worse. He watched as she grabbed her phone off of the nightstand that stood on the side of the bed. Standing over her, he was able to see that her screen saver was a picture of her and her child.

Eternity was smiling while tickling the baby. His chocolate skin glistened from the flash of the camera, and his dimples deepened with his smile. Eternity wiped the tears from her face with one hand while she unlocked her phone with the other. *Damn, I gotta get her kid back.* He felt for her because he knew that she was a mother suffering the absolute worse pain, the not knowing where your child is. He had heard of the gut pain that came with that feeling. He knew that when he finally had children that he would never be subject to that kind of pain because the protection of his children will be at the top of his priority list.

She gave Bleek the number, and he took his phone out of his pocket to dial it. He hovered over the green button to call. The conversation he was about to have if the call was even answered, he didn't want to have in front of her. While still on the dial pad, he locked his phone and then put it back in his jacket. He quickly put his sneakers back on.

"Where are you going?" She asked with the sniffle.

"I need to make sure my boy is good in the living room. I'm not leaving. We gone get your baby back, E. I promise. Any nigga that plays with kids is a dead nigga in my book. Especially his own kid it's just—"

He stopped speaking when he saw tears fill Eternity's eyes again. He walked over to her and then kissed the top of her head. She was gasping for air, and just with one word, he leveled her.

"Breathe…" – he waited for her to control her breathing before he continued— "you trust me?" he asked.

He tilted his head to the side to look her directly in the face.

"Yes," she whispered.

"Then know that I got this."

Gently he kissed her snot covered lips. He wiped his mouth before he exited the room.

Walking into the living room, he saw that Man-Man and Sha were engaged in small talk. Sports. That was the go-to topic of conversation when men were around new men. The topic of sports was an even playing field for most men. Sha, not knowing the kind of man that Man-Man was wouldn't dare talk street shit.

Unknowingly to him, the man that sat in the chair across from him was just as street as they came.

"Where's Tori?" Bleek asked, interrupting the conversation. He needed to know everything that there was to know about Vincent; he figured that no one other than Tori could give him the information that he needed.

"I sent her to go and lie down, all of this is stressing the hell out of her, and it's no good for my baby."

Bleek understood. If he was put in Man-Man's shoes, he would want his lady to be stress-free while carrying his child as well. He sighed and then took a seat on the couch next to Sha. Once he found a spot of comfort, Man-Man opened his mouth.

"I drove around everywhere last night. I couldn't find this nigga anywhere."

"You know where he normally be?" Bleek asked. Man-Man had his interest.

"Well yeah, he's like my cousin."

Bleek leaned up to sit on the edge of the chair, and so did Man-Man. Where most men feared Bleek, Man-Man didn't. It was the thoroughness in him that was embedded in his bones. He taught himself to fear no one, especially another man that bled just as he did. He could feel the tension in his room under his roof because of his last statement, but it was already said.

"Mmm," Bleek grumbled as he caressed his beard.

It was taking everything in him not to pull his weapon from his waistband and put two into Man-Man's head. Just off affiliation to Bleek, Man-Man was guilty. Just as guilty as Vincent just because they were kin or *like cousins*. Bleek didn't care. Anyone connected to Vincent in any way was a target to him, and he never missed his targets. Tori entered the room and just at the right moment. Sensing the tension in the room, she took a seat on Man-Man's lap.

While walking down the stairs, she caught the ending of their conversation. She heard the part that Man-Man said about him and Vincent being family. She knew Bleek well, all too well. So, she knew that the only thing that was keeping her man alive was her. The loyalty and love that he had for Eternity would ensure that her sister was safe. That olive branch extended down to Man-Man without him even knowing it.

"So, that's your cousin…" Bleek's spade nose flared as he said the statement, but then he gained self-control, "where would he go to get low?"

"Vee has always been secretive, so to be a hunnit with you. I don't know. Today I'm gonna go by the old hood where we grew up to see if anyone saw him. I even went to his baby mama house and she ain't heard from him. I'm putting my lines of loyalty out here right now. This my lady right here and in that room back there her sister is hurting something crazy. Childhood friend or not… this shit is unforgivable. So, if he gotta go, then so be it."

Bleek listened to Man-Man talk. To the regular man, what Man-Man had said would have been reassuring, but Bleek didn't give two shits about it. In his life, he had seen what looked to be the most loyal soldiers fold on the same men that were responsible for how they ate. Words were just that to Bleek, actions meant everything to him, and he knew that if given the opportunity to pull the trigger on his "cousin" that Man-Man wouldn't do it.

"There are no ifs in that statement… when I see him, he's dead."

The look in Bleek's eyes was stone cold. On the inside, Man-Man chuckled because he could already see that Bleek was thorough. Under the next man's roof, he was respectively flexing, and he didn't even try hard when he did it. Bleek sat back on the couch. Still, he wasn't relaxed but he wouldn't be as visibly guarded in front of Man-Man.

"Okay, so what's the plan? How can I help?" Man-Man asked.

"Still go by y'all old hood and get any information that you can on him. I have his number. I'm just waiting until tonight to give him a call. I'm not trynna have a shoot out in broad daylight, and I already know that is how it will end. It's obvious that he's holding their kid in exchange for me."

Man-Man nodded his head up and down as he listened. He tapped Tori's leg so that she could stand, and then he stood.

"I'll be back," he said to Tori just before he kissed the top of her head.

He was confident enough to know that Vincent wouldn't visit his home. He knew that Vincent knew that besides Man-Man being a good shot, his home held enough arsenal to cover him if a zombie apocalypse ever hit.

"Aye bae, order food or something. I don't want you on your feet."

Man-Man said just before he walked out of the front door.

Chapter 14

Man-Man walked to the end of his driveway and then got into Tori's G-Wagon. She hated for him to drive her car because he always moved her seat, but she always blocked his vehicle in with hers in the driveway. He stood on the outside of the car as he held onto the button to push her chair back.

When the chair wouldn't go back anymore, he got into the car and then closed the door behind him. He backed out of the driveway and then made his way out east. It had been a while since he had been in the neighborhood where he had grown up. He didn't have ties there anymore. With his mother dying from cancer and then his father getting gunned down a few years after that, he had no reason to be there. The only thing he was loyal to there was his barber, and then that changed when he married Nova and bought the house that he was living in now.

His home was a little way from his old barber, so he ended up finding another one closer to his home that was more convenient for him. He made a left onto Wilcox Boulevard and drove down for about five minutes until he made a right and pulled into a lot. He was prepping himself to hear the verbal beating he would get from his old barber, the establishment's owner. He hopped out of the truck and then closed the door behind him.

The wind outside caused him to zip up his puffer Galarché jacket as he walked to the shop.

"Ohhh, look what the cool chill brought in."

The barber closest to the front door said as soon as Man-Man walked in. He put his clippers down and then rounded the chair that his client was in.

Man-Man embraced the older man as he smiled.

"Ahhh, you clowning already, huh?" Man-Man asked as he patted the older man's back with the embrace.

"What ya walked in here for? You finally coming back to the nigga that gave you a hairline, to begin with?" the barber asked as Man-Man took a seat in one of the chairs that were alongside the front door.

"Na old man, I just got a shape up a little while ago." Man-Man said as he ran his hand over his auburn colored hair.

"So, what brings you by?"

The barber asked as he picked up the blade and then finished getting to work on his client.

"Charles… you saw my cousin around here?" Man-Man got straight to the point.

Charles closed the razor that he was just using to sharpen his client's edges and then quickly cleaned the man's face and edges with alcohol. He unbuttoned the cape from the man's neck and then waited for his payment. As soon as the man gave him the money, Charles waited for him to exit before he responded.

"I haven't seen Vee in years. I'ma say the last time I saw him was the year that ya daddy died."

Man-Man wrinkled his nose at the mention of his father. Still, such a touchy subject he hated when he was brought up. But he knew Charles long enough, he was his barber from when he was a boy, and before that, he used to tend to his father's head.

Charles snapped his fingers like he had just remembered something.

"What I can say is that just yesterday, when I stepped outside to have me a cigarette, I thought I saw his car parked out there in the lot. You know I heard he riding around in a yellow mustang, he the only nigga out here with one too. He probably was in the hardware store just next door. But then again, I could be mistaken because the car done had a baby seat in the back and I know that all of Vee's kids are school-aged."

Man-Man's eyes lit up at the mention of Vincent's car. He rubbed his stubble beard and then rose from his seat. There were about three hours until sundown, so he knew that he had to think quickly.

"Thanks, old man." He said to Charles as he went to embrace him again.

"Mm-hmm now don't wait until you need something to bring ya ass round here. You can start coming by just to check-in." Charles touched Man-Man's shoulder, "I mean it," he added.
Man-Man gave him a weak smile and then walked out of the barbershop.

The drive back to his home, he thought of the only two places that Vincent could have been. They had a trap house that was not too far from the barber's and then Vincent had an income property that was only a few miles away as well. As Man-Man drove home, he thought about the income property that he had put his cousin on to. Since Eternity had gotten into her accident, Vincent had expressed his thoughts about leaving the game alone and solely focusing on the income of legit businesses. Man-Man explained to him that the best way for him to make his money was for him to start flipping homes.

When Man-Man had first left the game, that was his primary source of income, when he got enough money up, that's when he started co-owning companies and then later, he opened his own sports bar. *He gotta be at that income property.* He thought to himself as he took his cellphone out of his coat pocket. Just to be sure, he called one of his old workers who was responsible for the trap house that was in that area.

"Yo," the man answered on the first ring.

"Big Dre, you saw Vee round there?"

"Nope... his day to pick up was yesterday too. His ass ain't come round here."

"Aight thanks," Man-Man ended the line.

Then is when he knew that his cousin had to be housed up in the income property. He hated that things had to come to this. The same man that he could lean on after his father's demise had to go. All because of clouded judgment. Still, Man-Man wasn't giving the full story on the paternity of Eternity's child. He had no idea that everything had to do with Bleek and Vincent but in his mind, there was nothing in the world that would make him risk the health of an innocent child. *He probably just trynna scare her ass,* he thought as he pulled into his driveway.

He saw Bleek standing outside on the front porch. He watched as Bleek pulled out his phone. Man-Man sighed when he noticed that the sun was starting to set. It was t-minus two hours to game time. A piece of him wanted to sit this one out, but he knew that he couldn't. Tori would never let him hear the end of it if he did.

"Fuck," he mumbled under his breath as he exited the car.

Bleek pulled his phone out of his pocket and then watched as the G-Wagon pulled into the driveway. He had his thumb hovered over the number that Eternity had given him. He had just left the room that she had herself locked away in. Because of him, she finally had eaten. It had been almost 48 hours since her last meal, but she didn't care. Her mind wasn't fixated on food. She was too preoccupied with worrying about the welfare of her child. Bleek sighed as he thought of the mess that he voluntarily put himself in.

Only for her would he be ready to go to war. He put his emotions on the front line for her always, and this is why he requested the presence of Sha. Having his right-hand man at his side was mandatory, he knew that the only two people in the world that would check him on his emotions were Ty and Sha. Being that he didn't want to put Ty in any line of fire because he had a family to live for, he settled on Sha.

A great settlement at that because he was groomed for the streets. He came to the table as a skilled hustler and killer. When Bleek noticed that Man-Man was taking longer than expected to get out of the car, he decided to make that call. Still uneasy, he held his thumb hovered over the green call button on his screen.

Since he had touched down in Chattanooga, Eternity constantly called Vincent's number. It did nothing but ring out. She even Facetimed Vincent, and that too did nothing but ring out. That by itself pissed Bleek off. He knew that Vincent was taunting her. He could have blocked her number but instead, he wanted her to suffer. With every ring in Eternity's ear, Bleek knew that it was agonizing pain for her. She held anticipation with each ring. Bleek had to take her cellphone from her to get her to stop calling. He tilted his head from left to right to crack his neck and then he pressed the call button.

The phone only rang in his ear twice before someone picked up. Bleek listened to the silence.

"Hmmm," he heard a man chuckle in his ear, *"a damn Florida number calling me. Little ol me, so you must be this Malik cat, huh?"*

"You know exactly who this is, and time isn't something that I enjoy wasting so, this is how this will go. You're going to tell me exactly where you are, you are going to give her back her baby and then me and you can chat."

"Chat? I ain't bouta chat whiff you. Nigga, this bigger than a chat."

"It's not. You're an insecure nigga that wanna play on a real nigga field so bad. You should have done your homework when it came to me. Now, where are you?" Bleek said into the phone.

There was an eerie silence. Bleek watched as Man-Man started to exit the car. Vincent chuckled before he responded.

"Yea... I did do my homework, Malik Browne. That's why I ain't telling you shit. You big Spanish affiliated, right? Come and find ya bwoy. Oh... find me before midnight or I'm killing ha kid." Anger caused Bleek's nose to crinkle. He hated niggas like Vincent. He could tell that Vincent was the kind of man that would disassociate himself with his own blood all because of what he and a female were going through. Weak ass, weak-minded, bitter ass men. When you're a father and a real father, that should NEVER be the case.

"You would kill your own blood because you're salty that you been a rebound?" Bleek asked.

Man-Man locked eyes with Bleek and then mouthed *"I got the location"* to him. Bleek shook his head up and down as he held the phone to his ear.

"I said midnight."

Vincent said just before the line ended in Bleek's ear. By then, Man-Man was in talking distance.

"Where is he?" Bleek asked, getting straight to the point.

"Let's go inside and talk about this."

Man-Man led the way into his home, and then Bleek followed.

"What's the word?" Sha asked as soon as he noticed that the two men had entered the room.

Without even turning around, he knew exactly when they had walked in. So thorough, he was always on point and that went for everywhere that he went. Man-Man looked down at his coffee table and saw that guns, clips and bullets were scattered around.

"Y'all think y'all have enough artillery," Man-Man joked.

Bleek and Sha looked at him with straight faces.

"Where is he?" Bleek asked the same question that he had asked when they were standing on the porch.

"I think—"

"You think?" Bleek questioned, "you just told me that you have the location. I don't have time for thinks when I'm not on familiar turf. What's stopping me from putting a hot one in you right fucking now?"

Bleek had no more patience. He was ready to go to war.

"Well, for starters by the time you reach down to the table or reach into ya back waistline to get your gun, I been done got one-off."

Bleek was impressed he never disclosed that he was currently carrying, but he knew that Man-Man would be a fool to think otherwise.

"Now, you think what?" Bleek asked with a grin.
He liked the attitude of the man in front of him. Intimidation didn't sway him even with him being obviously outnumbered. *This Chris Brown looking ass nigga got some heart,* Bleek thought as he slowly took a seat next to Sha.

"He has to be inside of one of his income properties. It's not too far from here. It's located in the same neighborhood where we had grown up. It's a ranch-style home. Two bedrooms, front and back yard."

"Do you think he has men with him?" Bleek asked.

"He would be a damn fool not to have any. What I can say is that if he does, there's not a lot of them. His men are my men, and being that I didn't get any calls, I can guarantee you that he only told his loyal workers about this. That's probably only about five niggas."
Man-Man stopped speaking and then twisted his mouth in thought.

"Shit... if he back on Heavenz, I don't know what to expect." Man-Man honestly admitted.

"Heavenz?" Bleek questioned.

"That's them pills, right? I heard if you get hooked on them that the trip is worse than K2." Sha chimed in.

"Yea, that's them," Man-Man confirmed.

Bleek shook his head because he hated that the conversation was getting off-topic.

"Aight… I say we pull out in an hour." Bleek said to navigate the conversation back on track.

Man-Man started to climb the stairs until Bleek spoke.

"Tori is inside of the room with E."

"Good looking."

Man-Man stepped down the three steps that he had started to climb and then made his way to the bedroom that was located on the first floor. The door to the room was cracked.

"Please sis, stop crying. Bleek is here, and you know he will get him back. You want to know how I'm getting by?"
He heard Tori say.

There was a pause, and then he heard her start talking again.

"I feel like Vincent is acting out. He can't take that in-between y'all story; there is a Bleek. I tell myself, sis, that he would not hurt that baby. Vincent may be a lot of things, but I don't think he would hurt any of his kids."

"That's not his kid…" Man-Man heard Eternity whisper.
He leaned his head closer to the door because he could have sworn that he had heard wrong.

"Sis we don't know that you never got the test don—"

"I did…"

"What?"

Man-Man could hear the confusion in Tori's voice.

He leaned up against the hallway wall outside of the room as he listened. He couldn't believe what his ears were hearing.

"My last week in the hospital I had the test done. One night when Vincent stayed the night in my room, I swabbed his mouth. I told the doctors to mail the results to the house because I didn't want them giving me results there at the hospital where Vincent barely left me on my own. I got the results in the mail yesterday before we went out."

Man-Man heard Eternity's voice crack before she started talking again.

"This is why I asked you to watch him last night. I was going to tell Vincent and then leave, I swear. Sis... I... was... going to leave."

Eternity started to cry, so Tori pulled her into her arms.

"Did you get a chance to tell Bleek yet," Tori asked.

"No..."

Shit, Man-Man thought to himself when Eternity finished talking. Now he knew that things were way deeper. He understood why Bleek was currently involved.

Knock, knock

He lightly knocked on the door.

"Come in," he heard Tori say.

Slowly, he pushed open the door.

"We about to leave." He said as soon as he walked in.

Eternity got out of the bed and then slowly limped over to the window. In the windowsill was her medical boot. She took a seat in the windowsill and then pulled her leg over the other. She put her foot into the boot and then strapped the Velcro straps over the top of her foot.

"Y'all not coming," Man-Man said.

"I understand why Tori can't come. I, on the other hand, am coming. I need to come. I need to make sure that my baby is okay." Man-Man opened his mouth to argue with her, but Bleek spoke from behind him.

"She's right. She does need this. When I walk your son out of that house, you need to be the first one there to hold him."

Eternity looked over Man-Man's shoulder at Bleek.

"Are we in your van, or are we taking two cars?" Man-Man turned around and asked Bleek.

"We need to take two cars. You and E can be in a car and me and my boy will be in the van. I thank you for giving me this information, but you don't need to be in that crib, either. He is still your family."

Without saying another word, Bleek turned to exit.

Everyone else in the room followed him to the front of the house. Sha was putting the guns into a duffle bag when everyone joined him in the room. He zipped the bag shut and then tossed it over his shoulder. He was the first to leave the house. Bleek waited in the hall for Eternity. He helped her walk to the front door.

"I love you," Tori said to Man-Man as she kissed him repeatedly on his lips.

"I love you," he whispered to her in between kisses. He rubbed her belly and then crouched down to be level with her small baby bump.

"I love you," he whispered to her stomach.

"Okay, Marcelo, you're being mushy," she pushed him away from her, "just go and then make it back home to me," Tori said

"I always make it home to you." He said to her. He was walking backward while still facing her, he winked his eye at her and then went out the front door.

He could see that Bleek was putting Eternity into the G-wagon he had gotten out of earlier. He pulled his gun from his back waistband and then pressed the ejection button on the side of the clip. When Man-Man saw that his clip was full, he inserted the clip back into the gun and then put it back. He always kept one in the head, so he knew that as soon as he took his gun off safety that he would be ready to go.

He stood on the sidelines as he watched the encounter between Bleek and Eternity. Repeatedly Bleek kissed the top of her head. He could tell that Eternity was crying because he saw Bleek wiping her cheeks. *Damn, this nigga really about to go to war for her, and he doesn't know that's his kid,* Man-Man thought.

He turned away from their encounter to give them their real privacy. Being that he was about to be a first-time father, he looked at the world differently. If no one wanted to put a bullet in Vincent, he did. The simple fact that his cousin would even toy with the attempt to put a child in harm's way had him ready to let one go right in between Vincent's eyes. Silence him for life for even thinking that it was okay to threaten the life of a child. End him forever for even playing with the thought.

"You know the address by heart to give it to me?" Bleek asked, breaking Man-Man from his thoughts.

"Yea..." he gave Bleek the address.

Bleek put the address into his phone and then began to walk off.

"Yo, Bleek," Man-Man called out.

Without saying a word, Bleek turned around. Man-Man just looked at him. He toyed with the idea of telling him what he had overheard. Suddenly, he decided against it because he knew that emotions would cloud his judgment. If everything that Tori had told Man-Man about Bleek was true, then he knew that he was thorough. Dropping a bomb like this before this move would alter how he would move in the situation.

With emotions and clouded judgment, second-guesses came into play. The last thing that he wanted to do was risk Bleek's life off information that wasn't even his to disclose.

"When we get there I'ma park a few houses down just in case he's looking out the window or something."
Bleek nodded his head and then made his way to the van. Sha pulled off of the block as soon as Bleek got into the car. Man-Man backed out of the driveway and then followed behind them.

Chapter 15

"Arrived."

Siri's voice-activated the stealth mode in Bleek, he leaned up in the chair and then pulled his gun from his waistband. He opened the glove compartment on his side and grabbed his silencer. Quickly he screwed it onto the end of his snub. He passed the other muffler to Sha and then he quickly did the same. Bleek's phone vibrated in his pocket. Figuring that it was Eternity wanting to know an update, he pulled his phone out of his pocket. He looked down at the screen and saw Paris' name. He quickly ignored the call and then got his head back in the game.

"Everything good?" Sha asked.

"Yea…"

Bleek responded as he looked at every window of the house. When he didn't see any movement, he got out of the car. Headlights flashed twice against the side of the house. He knew that it had to be Man-Man telling him that he was nearby. Slowly he walked towards the front of the house.

"Take the back," Bleek whispered to Sha.

Without saying a word, Sha did what he was told. Something felt off to Bleek. *Where's his men?* He wondered as he slowly walked towards the front of the house. Thinking of the innocent child that was involved, he pushed past his worries and continued forward.

When he reached the front door, he put his ear to the frame and listened. The sound of a baby crying could be heard. *Fuck,* he thought. He took his gloved hand and turned the knob. The gut-wrenching signs only intensified when he discovered that the door was open. He was met with darkness.

Bang…. Bang…

Two shots rang off, which caused Bleek to find concealment behind the wall in the foyer. He knew that he was being shot at when the bullets whizzed past his head. He sent two shots to the shadowy figure that sat in a chair by the back patio door.

Pstt…. Pstt…

His muffled shots, due to his silencer, hissed inside of the darkroom. He took cover behind the wall again and then breathed deeply. When he peeked around the wall, he knew that he was now alone in the house. The patio door in the back was wide open which allowed the darkness skylight to peek into the home. Bleek used this to his advantage by quickly flicking on a light switch that was nearby.

Bang... Bang...
Bang...

Bleek paused; those shots were coming from outside. He knew that Sha had a silencer on his gun so, for Bleek to hear gunshots, he knew that his homeboy's direction was the target. From the front door to the back one, he turned from left to right. With his gun in hand, he carefully cleared the space. Like a trained officer, he searched to make sure that he was truly alone. The light he turned on in the front of the house didn't stretch all the way to the back.

Yet again, he was in darkness. It was then that he realized that the baby crying had stopped. *Did he run out with the baby?* He wondered as he drew his attention to the dark figure that was still seated in the chair. He tucked his gun closer to his chest. Still, with it pointed outward and his finger on the trigger he slowly walked towards the figure. He pulled his cellphone out of his back pocket and then flashed light onto the figure.

"What the fuck?" He whispered to himself as he tried to make sense of what he was looking at.

A man with green eyes and a low cut was duct-taped to the chair. His mouth was taped as well. Bleek looked into the man's lifeless eyes. The dried tear stains that ran down his face was an indication that he was crying. Most likely pleading for his life. Bleek's eyes traveled down to the man's chest when he noticed that there were straps on both of his shoulders. Instantly, his stomach went hallow. The man had a baby sling attached to his body and in the sling was a child.

"Shitttt!" Bleek hissed as he put his gun and phone away. He rushed over to the baby and then quickly unstrapped him from the dead man. Bleek knew that the body that the baby was attached to wasn't fresh because rigor mortis had started to set in. He felt the stiffness of the course when he removed the baby from the harness. As he held the child firmly, he could feel the blood soaking his black T-shirt.

"Shittttt!"

He found the source and saw that the baby was hit in the leg. *He didn't stop crying until I started shooting. I had to do this.* Bleek's thoughts caused him to head for the back-patio door without thinking first. At that moment, he didn't care what war was being waged outside of that door. He needed to get Eternity's son to the hospital.

"Come on, little man. I know you're strong like ya moms. Come on..." Bleek whispered as he applied pressure to the infant's thigh.

Bleek was grateful that when he had taken his two shots that he was aiming center mass. Had he been aiming for the head, he knew that he would have ended the boy's life. Although the breathing in his arms was faint, it was there. Bleek had hopes that her son would make it; they just had to make it to a hospital first. He walked out of the back door and then halted at the scene before him.

"Sha, what happened?" Bleek calmly asked as he tried his hardest to analyze the scene before him.

A bald head man was laid out on the grass. He had lifeless eyes that looked up at the stars. Bleek's eyes rolled over to Sha. *What the fuck is he doing out here?* Bleek wondered when he looked at the man that Sha was aiding.

"I don't know where he came from. It was just that nigga and me shooting out," – Sha nodded his head in the direction of the bald-headed man on the lawn, then he turned his attention back to the man beneath him – "and then… I really don't know where the fuck he came from." Sha stuttered out as he applied pressure to the man's neck that was on the floor next to him.

There was so much blood that Bleek could see it seeping through Sha's closed fingers. *What the fuck is he doing out here?* Bleek thought again…

To be continued…

** Leave those reviews **

C. Wilson

Follow C. Wilson on social media

Instagram: @authorcwilson

Facebook: @CelesteWilson

Join my reading group on Facebook: Cecret Discussionz

Follow my reading group on Instagram:

@CecretDiscussionz

Twitter: @Authorcwilson_

Tell me what you think of this story in a customer review.

Thank you,

-xoxo-

C. Wilson

Made in the USA
Columbia, SC
09 February 2025